Spooky Stories

For Adults

Crafted by Skriuwer

Introduction

In the darkest corners of our world, where the light of hope seldom reaches, there are forces at work that feed on the fears, sorrows, and regrets of the human soul. These forces take many forms—some are the nightmares that haunt us in the dead of night, others are the whispers in the shadows that drive us to the brink of madness. They are the embodiment of despair, ancient and relentless, and they have claimed countless victims throughout the ages.

The stories within this collection are tales of those who have encountered these malevolent entities, beings that exist beyond our understanding, creatures that thrive on the pain and suffering of their prey. Each story unfolds in a different setting—a remote town plagued by a creature that drives its victims to suicide, a monster that lurks in the shadows of a small community, a demonic presence in a desecrated church, a monstrous force that preys on a town's deepest fears. And in each story, the characters face an unimaginable terror that tests the limits of their courage, sanity, and will to survive.

These are not tales of heroes who overcome the odds, nor of triumphant victories over evil. Instead, they are stories of struggle, of the human spirit pushed to its breaking point, of the thin line between hope and despair. The monsters in these tales are not easily defeated, for they are not just physical beings—they are the darkness that resides within all of us, the inescapable shadow that lurks just beyond the edge of reason.

As you read these stories, prepare yourself to journey into the heart of darkness, where the line between reality and nightmare is blurred, and where the only certainty is that nothing is as it seems. The characters you will meet are ordinary people, thrust into extraordinary circumstances, battling forces they cannot comprehend. And as you follow their descent into madness, you may find yourself questioning the nature of fear, the power of despair, and the true cost of survival.

So turn the page, if you dare, and step into a world where the shadows hold more than just darkness, where the monsters are real, and where the end is never as simple as it seems. But be warned: once you enter these stories, there may be no turning back, for the shadows have a way of claiming those who linger too long.

Shadows of the Forgotten

Chapter 1

The Old Manor

James Carter stood at the entrance of the old manor, the massive wooden doors creaking ominously as he pushed them open. The air was thick with dust and the scent of decay, a stark contrast to the crisp autumn air outside. He hesitated for a moment, feeling a chill that had nothing to do with the weather. This was the place he had inherited from a distant relative—a place he had never known existed until a week ago.

James was a historian, drawn to the secrets of the past. His fascination with local legends had brought him here, to this crumbling mansion on the outskirts of a small, almost forgotten town. He had decided to spend the night, documenting his findings for what he hoped would be his next book.

The interior of the manor was a snapshot of a bygone era. Dusty portraits lined the walls, their eyes seeming to follow James as he moved through the dimly lit hallways. He set up his camera and notebook in the grand foyer, determined to capture every detail. As he walked, the floorboards groaned under his weight, each step echoing through the empty halls.

Exploring further, James found old photographs and journals, their pages yellowed and brittle with age. Each room he entered seemed to have its own story, its own secrets. He spent hours sifting through the remnants of the past, uncovering a dark history of the manor. It had been the site of numerous disappearances and unexplained deaths over the years.

As the sun dipped below the horizon, the manor took on a more sinister appearance. Shadows seemed to stretch and shift, and the temperature dropped noticeably. James brushed off the cold as a natural result of the old building, but the hairs on the back of his neck stood on end. He heard whispers that seemed to come from nowhere, and the creaking of the house felt more like footsteps than the groans of an old structure.

Determined to press on, he discovered a hidden door in the library, concealed behind a tall bookshelf. It led to a narrow staircase descending into darkness. James hesitated, feeling a knot of unease tighten in his stomach. But his curiosity won out, and he began to descend, his flashlight cutting through the inky blackness.

Halfway down the stairs, he saw it—a fleeting shadow darting across the corner of his vision. He whipped his flashlight around, but saw nothing. His heart pounded as he continued down, finally reaching a heavy, locked door. It was secured with a rusted padlock, which seemed odd considering the apparent abandonment of the manor.

James searched the basement and found an old key ring hanging on a nail. After several attempts, he found the right key and unlocked the door. The basement room was unlike anything he had ever seen. The walls were covered in strange symbols and drawings, and the air was thick with the smell of old blood and burnt offerings. In the center of the room was a crude altar, stained with dark, dried blood.

He found a journal on the altar, its pages filled with accounts of dark rituals performed by his ancestors. The entries spoke of summoning spirits, of sacrifices made to appease some malevolent force that supposedly haunted the manor. The more he read, the more unsettled he became.

The journal detailed the final ritual performed to seal away a curse that had plagued the family for generations. The symbols on the walls were meant to contain whatever dark entity they had summoned. But the last entry was the most chilling. It warned that anyone who disturbed the symbols would unleash the curse once more.

As he read the final words, a cold wind swept through the room, extinguishing his flashlight. James felt a presence, a dark and malevolent force that seemed to press in on him from all sides. Panic set in, and he bolted for the stairs, stumbling in the dark.

He reached the top and tried to open the door to the foyer, but it wouldn't budge. He slammed his shoulder against it, but it felt as though it were sealed by an invisible force. The whispers grew louder, more insistent, and the shadows around him seemed to grow darker, more solid.

Desperation clawed at him as he remembered the journal's warning. He needed to restore the symbols, to seal away whatever he had unleashed. But as he turned to head back to the basement, he saw them—figures emerging from the shadows, their eyes glowing with an otherworldly light.

James screamed, backing away from the advancing figures. He felt a cold hand close around his wrist, pulling him back into the darkened manor. The last thing he saw was the front door slamming shut with a final, deafening crash.

Chapter 2

The Haunting Begins

James woke up with a start, his heart pounding in his chest. He was still inside the manor, lying on the cold, hard floor of the grand foyer. His mind raced as he tried to piece together what had happened. The oppressive sense of dread he had felt in the basement was now suffocating. Every breath was a struggle, and the air seemed thick with an unseen malevolence.

He stood up, his legs shaky, and tried the front door again. It was still locked, refusing to budge no matter how hard he pulled or pushed. Panic surged through him, and he ran to the windows, but they too were sealed shut, as if the house itself was determined to keep him inside.

James forced himself to stay calm. He needed to find another way out. He moved from room to room, but the manor seemed to have a mind of its own, leading him in circles. Hallways that should have led to the front of the house now led him deeper into its dark heart. He could hear the whispers again, louder and more insistent, as if they were urging him to give in to despair.

Objects began to move on their own. Chairs scraped across the floor, picture frames rattled on the walls, and doors slammed shut with no one near them. The whispers grew louder, a cacophony of voices that seemed to come from every direction. James felt eyes on him, watching his every move.

He saw his first ghostly apparition in the dining room—a woman in a tattered dress, her eyes hollow and lifeless. She reached out to him, her mouth moving as if she were speaking, but no sound came out. James backed away, his skin crawling with fear. He turned and fled, but everywhere he went, more apparitions appeared. They were trapped souls, bound to the manor by the same curse that now ensnared him.

James could feel the presence of the malevolent entity growing stronger. It was feeding off his fear, growing more powerful with each passing moment. He needed to understand what it wanted, why it was haunting him, and how he could stop it.

Desperate for answers, James began to search for a way to communicate with the spirits. He found an old Ouija board in one of the dusty parlors and set it up on a table. His hands shook as he placed them on the planchette, summoning the courage to ask his questions.

"Who are you?" he asked aloud. The planchette moved, spelling out the name "Eleanor." He felt a chill run down his spine. Eleanor was one of the names he had seen in the journals. She had been a victim of the rituals, sacrificed to the entity that haunted the manor.

"What do you want?" James asked. The planchette moved again, spelling out "Freedom." The spirits were trapped, bound to the manor by the dark rituals performed by his ancestors.

As the session continued, James learned more about his family's dark past. They had made a pact with the entity, summoning it to gain power and wealth. But the entity had turned on them, cursing the family and binding their souls to the manor. The only way to break the curse was to banish the entity once and for all.

James felt a cold draft and turned to see the entity standing in the doorway. It was a dark, shadowy figure with glowing red eyes that seemed to bore into his soul. The entity spoke, its voice a low, guttural growl.

"Your family owes me a debt," it said. "They summoned me, and now I will have my revenge."

James felt a surge of anger. "What do you want from me?" he demanded.

"I want what was promised to me," the entity replied. "Your family's souls are mine. And now, so is yours."

James knew he had to find a way to stop the entity before it consumed him. He remembered the journal's warnings about the symbols and the rituals. There had to be a way to use them to banish the entity, but it would not be easy.

Gathering his courage, James decided to confront the entity. He raced back to the basement, the shadows seeming to close in around him. He found the journal and began to read the rituals, searching for a way to banish the entity.

The entity followed him, its presence growing stronger. It summoned the spirits of the manor, turning them against James. He fought his way through the basement, dodging the grasping hands of the spirits and the flying objects hurled by the entity's power.

He found the ritual he was looking for—a banishment spell that required a sacrifice. James realized with a sinking heart that the sacrifice needed to be him. He had to give his life to break the curse and free the trapped souls.

With trembling hands, he began the ritual, chanting the words from the journal. The entity roared in anger, its form shifting and writhing as it tried to stop him. The spirits surrounded James, their faces filled with hope and desperation.

As he completed the ritual, a blinding light filled the basement. The entity screamed, its form dissolving into the light. The spirits began to fade, their souls finally freed from the curse. James felt a searing pain as the ritual took its toll, and darkness closed in around him.

Chapter 3

The Aftermath

James woke up in complete darkness. He lay still for a moment, disoriented and unsure if he was alive or dead. The air was cold, and the only sound was the faint echo of his own breathing. He slowly sat up, his body aching from the confrontation with the entity. As his eyes adjusted to the darkness, he realized he was in a place unlike any he had ever seen.

The atmosphere was oppressive, filled with an eerie whispering that seemed to come from everywhere and nowhere at once. Shadows flickered around him, their movements unnatural and unsettling. He took a deep breath and stood up, trying to find his bearings. The floor beneath him felt solid, but the world around him was shrouded in an impenetrable gloom.

James began to walk, his footsteps echoing in the darkness. He called out, but his voice was swallowed by the void. He didn't know where he was or how he had gotten there, but one thing was clear: this place was not of the living world.

As he wandered through the darkness, James encountered other souls, their forms faint and ghostly. They looked at him with a mixture of curiosity and fear. He approached one of them, a young woman who seemed less faded than the others.

"Where am I?" James asked, his voice trembling.

The woman shook her head. "We are in the Realm of the Lost," she said. "This is where the souls bound by the curse are trapped."

James felt a chill run down his spine. "Is there a way out?" he asked, desperate for any hope.

The woman looked around nervously. "There are dangers here," she whispered. "The shadows... they are not just shadows. The entity you faced in the manor, it controls this place. It feeds off our fear and despair."

James felt a surge of determination. He had to find a way out, not just for himself, but for all the souls trapped here.

Determined to escape, James continued his search, trying to find anything that could help him. He stumbled upon remnants of past rituals etched into the ground, symbols that glowed faintly in the dark. They looked similar to the ones he had seen in the manor, and he hoped they might hold the key to his escape.

As he studied the symbols, the air grew colder, and he felt a familiar presence. The malevolent entity appeared before him, its form even more terrifying than before. It was a monstrous shadow with glowing red eyes, its presence filling James with dread.

"You cannot escape," the entity hissed. "This realm is mine, and so are you."

James backed away, but the entity followed, its form shifting and writhing. He knew he had to act quickly if he wanted to survive.

The entity's true form was a nightmarish sight, a mass of darkness that seemed to absorb all light. James realized that it had been feeding off the souls trapped in the realm, growing more powerful with each one it consumed.

With no other choice, James decided to use the remnants of the rituals he had found. He began to trace the symbols on the ground, chanting the words he had memorized from the journal. The entity roared in anger, its form flickering as the symbols began to glow brighter.

"You think you can defeat me?" the entity snarled. "You are nothing but a mortal."

James ignored the taunts and continued the ritual, drawing on every ounce of his strength. The symbols glowed brighter, and the entity began to weaken, its form flickering and shrinking.

Realizing that he needed more power, James called out to the other souls. "Help me!" he shouted. "We can banish it together!"

The souls gathered around him, their forms growing more solid as they joined in the ritual. Together, they chanted the ancient words, their voices rising in a crescendo. The entity screamed in fury, its form dissolving into a swirling vortex of darkness.

James knew what he had to do. The final part of the ritual required a sacrifice, and he was willing to give his life to free the trapped souls. With a final, desperate chant, he completed the ritual, feeling his own life force being drained away.

As the last words left his lips, the vortex exploded in a blinding flash of light. The entity was banished, its screams fading into nothingness. The souls began to ascend, their forms turning to light as they were finally freed.

James fell to the ground, his vision fading. He felt a sense of peace, knowing that he had done what he had to do. As darkness closed in, he hoped that the curse was finally broken, and that the manor would be at peace.

Chapter 4

The Return

James woke up to the beeping sound of machines and the sterile scent of antiseptic. He blinked against the harsh fluorescent lights and tried to make sense of his surroundings. He was in a hospital bed, hooked up to various monitors. Confusion washed over him as he struggled to remember how he got here.

A nurse entered the room, noticing that he was awake. "You're awake! That's a miracle," she said, her eyes wide with astonishment. "We thought we lost you."

James tried to speak, but his throat was dry. The nurse handed him a glass of water, and he drank it gratefully. "What happened?" he croaked.

"You were found unconscious in that old manor," she explained. "The authorities brought you here, but... you were declared dead at the scene. Somehow, you came back."

James's mind raced. The last thing he remembered was completing the ritual to banish the entity. He had felt his life slipping away, and then... darkness. How was he alive?

As the days passed, James recovered physically, but his mind was haunted by memories of the dark realm and the entity. He couldn't shake the feeling that something was still wrong. Every time he closed his eyes, he saw the flickering shadows and heard the eerie whispers.

Strange things began to happen in the hospital. Lights flickered, cold spots appeared in his room, and he heard faint whispers that seemed to come from nowhere. James knew these were not coincidences. The entity's influence was still lingering.

He confided in the doctor, but they dismissed his concerns as symptoms of trauma and stress. James knew better. He had faced the entity before, and he could feel its presence creeping back into his life.

One afternoon, an elderly woman visited James. She introduced herself as Margaret, claiming to be a distant relative. She had a weathered face and eyes that seemed to hold centuries of knowledge.

"I came as soon as I heard what happened," she said, sitting beside his bed. "Our family has a dark history, and you were brave to face it."

James listened intently as Margaret recounted the history of the manor and the family curse. She explained how their ancestors had summoned the entity, binding it to the manor. Each generation had suffered because of it, and many had tried to break the curse, only to fail.

Margaret handed James a small talisman, an intricately carved piece of bone on a leather cord. "This will protect you," she said. "But be warned, the entity's power is strong. You must be careful."

James thanked her, feeling a renewed sense of purpose. He had to end this once and for all.

Determined to finish what he started, James returned to the manor. It looked worse than before, with broken windows and overgrown vegetation. The air was thick with a sense of foreboding, and the shadows seemed to writhe with malevolent intent.

Holding the talisman tightly, James entered the manor. The atmosphere was oppressive, and the whispers began almost immediately. The talisman glowed faintly, guiding him through the darkened halls.

As he moved deeper into the manor, he saw signs of recent supernatural activity: overturned furniture, deep scratches on the walls, and a lingering chill that seemed to seep into his bones. He knew he was getting closer to the source of the entity's power.

In the heart of the manor, James found a hidden chamber that he had not discovered before. The walls were covered with more ritualistic symbols, and in the center of the room was a stone altar. He knew this was the place where he could end the curse.

James prepared the final ritual, using the knowledge he had gained from the journals and the talisman for protection. As he chanted the ancient words, the air grew colder, and the shadows thickened.

The entity manifested before him, more monstrous than ever. Its form was a mass of writhing darkness with eyes that burned like embers. It roared in fury, shaking the very foundations of the manor.

James stood his ground, the talisman glowing brighter with each word of the chant. The entity lunged at him, but the talisman repelled it, burning it with a searing light.

With a final, desperate effort, James completed the ritual. The room was filled with a blinding light, and the entity screamed as it was pulled into the vortex. The ground shook, and the walls cracked, but James held firm, pouring all his strength into the ritual.

The light faded, and the room was silent. The entity was gone, banished forever. The talisman crumbled to dust in his hand, and James collapsed, exhausted but victorious.

Chapter 5

The Unexpected End

James returned to his modest home, his heart heavy but relieved. He had banished the entity and freed the trapped souls. For the first time in weeks, he allowed himself to relax. The familiar surroundings of his home were a welcome change from the horrors of the manor.

But as the days passed, subtle changes began to unsettle him. He noticed small things at first—objects slightly out of place, cold spots in rooms that had never felt chilly before. The feeling of being watched, which he had hoped to leave behind at the manor, began to creep back into his life.

James tried to dismiss these feelings as paranoia, remnants of the trauma he had endured. Yet, every night, as he lay in bed, he couldn't shake the sensation that unseen eyes were observing him from the shadows.

The strange occurrences grew more frequent and more disturbing. Books would fall from shelves without reason, lights would flicker despite being newly installed, and the whispers he thought he had silenced forever returned, more insistent and chilling than ever.

One evening, as he prepared for bed, he saw a ghostly apparition in the hallway. It was the same woman in the tattered dress, her hollow eyes staring at him with a silent plea. James's blood ran cold. He blinked, and she was gone, but the dread lingered.

The hauntings became relentless. Shadows moved of their own accord, and James could hear the faint echoes of the dark realm's whispers no matter where he was in the house. He realized, with growing horror, that he had not escaped the entity's grasp.

Desperate for answers, James began to search through his belongings for anything that could explain the resurgence of these horrors. He found an old family photograph, tucked away in a book he had brought back from the manor. The photograph showed his ancestors, gathered around the very altar where he had performed the banishment ritual.

As he examined the photograph closer, James noticed something that sent a chill down his spine. In the background, barely visible, was the shadowy form of the entity. It had been present in his family for generations, feeding off their fear and despair.

The realization hit him like a punch to the gut: the curse was never truly broken. The entity had simply latched onto him, using him as a conduit to escape the confines of the manor. Now it was free to haunt him anywhere, anytime.

The entity's manifestations grew bolder. It no longer confined itself to shadows and whispers. It began to appear as a dark, tangible presence in his home, its glowing red eyes filled with malice. James tried to use the knowledge from the journals to combat it, but each attempt was met with failure. The talisman was gone, and he had no other means of protection.

One night, as the entity loomed over him, it spoke. "You thought you could banish me?" it hissed. "I am bound to your bloodline, and now, I am bound to you."

James felt a deep, icy fear. The entity revealed its true plan: to use him as a vessel, to merge with his soul and take full control of his body. This would allow it to walk freely in the living world, spreading its curse and claiming more victims.

James fought with every ounce of his willpower to resist the entity's control. He barricaded himself in his room, trying to create a sanctuary from the encroaching darkness. But the entity was relentless, chipping away at his defenses both mental and physical.

He could feel its influence growing stronger, invading his thoughts, turning his own mind against him. Shadows seemed to crawl across his skin, whispers filled his ears, driving him to the brink of madness. Every attempt to banish it failed, and he realized with dawning horror that he was losing the battle.

In a last, desperate act, James tried to perform a final exorcism, drawing on all his remaining strength. But the entity was too powerful. It overpowered him, seizing control of his body with a triumphant roar.

James's consciousness faded, replaced by the cold, malevolent presence of the entity. As his own mind was swallowed by darkness, he knew he was lost. The entity, now in full control, looked through his eyes with a new sense of purpose.

It smiled with James's face, a chilling expression that bore no resemblance to his own. The entity was free, and with its new vessel, it would spread its curse far and wide. The horror that had haunted the Carter family for generations was just beginning.

The Blood Forest

Chapter 1

The Forest of Shadows

The sun was beginning to set as Sarah and Mark drove up the winding dirt road leading to the Forest of Shadows. Locals had told them tales of the ancient woods, shrouded in mystery and whispered legends. For Sarah, it was an opportunity to disconnect from the bustle of city life and reconnect with nature. Mark, on the other hand, saw it as a chance for adventure and to prove that there was no truth to the old superstitions.

They finally arrived at a small clearing near a serene lake, where they decided to set up camp. The forest loomed around them, the trees dense and imposing, their gnarled branches reaching out like skeletal fingers. The air was thick with the scent of pine and moss, but there was an underlying unease that neither could shake.

As they pitched their tent and gathered wood for a fire, the forest seemed to watch them, its silence almost deafening. Sarah tried to dismiss the feeling, focusing instead on the beauty of their surroundings. Mark was excited, eager to explore the uncharted paths and perhaps discover something new.

Night fell quickly, and with it, an eerie silence. The usual sounds of the forest—the chirping of crickets, the rustling of leaves—were conspicuously absent. The only sound was the crackling of their campfire, casting flickering shadows on the trees around them.

As they settled into their tent, Sarah heard a faint whispering, barely audible over the fire. She strained her ears, trying to make out the words, but they seemed to slip away just as she thought she could grasp them. Mark dismissed it as the wind, but Sarah couldn't shake the feeling that something was out there, watching them.

In the middle of the night, they were jolted awake by the sound of rustling outside their tent. Mark grabbed a flashlight and went out to investigate, leaving Sarah behind, her heart pounding in her chest. He scanned the area but saw nothing unusual. The forest was still and silent, as if holding its breath.

The next morning, they woke to a grisly sight. Around their campsite were the carcasses of small animals—rabbits, birds, and squirrels—arranged in a circle. Their bodies were mutilated, blood smeared across the ground in strange, ritualistic patterns. Sarah gasped, her hand flying to her mouth. Mark's face hardened as he inspected the macabre display.

"Someone's trying to scare us," Mark said, trying to sound confident. "It's probably just a sick prank."

But Sarah felt a deep unease settling over her. The forest, which had seemed so inviting in the daylight, now felt menacing. They decided to hike deeper into the woods, hoping to find other campers or some explanation for the gruesome discovery.

After hours of trekking through the dense undergrowth, they stumbled upon a dilapidated cabin. An old hermit emerged, his eyes wild and his beard long and tangled. He stared at them with a mixture of fear and pity.

"You shouldn't be here," he said, his voice a raspy whisper. "This forest is cursed. Blood rituals and vengeful spirits haunt these woods. Many have come, but few have left."

Mark scoffed at the old man's warnings, but Sarah felt a chill run down her spine. The hermit urged them to leave immediately, but Mark insisted on staying, determined to prove that there was nothing to fear.

As they walked away, the forest seemed to grow darker, the trees closing in around them. The air became thick and oppressive, and the sense of being watched intensified. Sarah clutched Mark's arm, her unease growing with each step.

As night fell once more, the forest came alive with terrifying sounds. The whispering returned, louder and more insistent, accompanied by rustling and snapping branches. Shadows moved just beyond the reach of their flashlight, darting between the trees.

Suddenly, they were attacked. Unseen forces ripped through the tent, slashing at them with invisible claws. Blood sprayed across the campsite as Mark and Sarah fought desperately to defend themselves. Mark screamed as something unseen dragged him into the darkness, his cries echoing through the forest.

Sarah stumbled back, her hands shaking and covered in blood. She could see movement in the shadows, eyes gleaming with malevolent intent. She realized with a sinking heart that they were not alone. The forest was alive with ancient, evil spirits, and they were hunting her.

Desperation gave her strength, and she grabbed a burning log from the fire, swinging it wildly to keep the shadows at bay. But the darkness was closing in, and the whispers grew louder, promising pain and death.

With no other choice, Sarah turned and ran, the forest seeming to twist and turn around her, every path leading deeper into the nightmare. She could feel the cold breath of the spirits on her neck, their claws reaching out to drag her into the shadows.

As she fled, she tripped over a root, falling hard to the ground. Pain shot through her ankle, and she cried out, scrambling to her feet. But it was too late. The shadows closed in, and the last thing she saw was the gleam of their eyes, filled with hunger and malice.

The forest consumed her screams, and silence fell once more. The Blood Forest had claimed another victim, and its ancient curse remained unbroken.

Chapter 2

The Survivors

Sarah awoke in darkness, her head throbbing and her body aching from the fall. The air was damp and cold, and she could hear the distant drip of water echoing through what sounded like a cavern. Panic surged through her as she realized she was underground, possibly in some old, forgotten cave system beneath the forest.

Her hands explored the ground around her, feeling the rough, cold stone and patches of damp earth. Her body was bruised and bloodied, and every movement sent waves of pain through her limbs. But she forced herself to sit up, gritting her teeth against the agony. She had to find a way out.

Using her hands to guide her in the pitch-black darkness, Sarah began to crawl, hoping to find some sign of an exit or at least a source of light. The cave was silent except for the occasional distant drip of water and her own labored breathing.

As she moved deeper into the cave, Sarah's eyes adjusted to the faint glow of bioluminescent fungi clinging to the walls. The eerie light revealed disturbing sights. Scattered around were remnants of previous victims: old, tattered clothes, personal items like watches and jewelry, and even skeletal remains. The bones were gnawed and broken, evidence of the horrific fate that had befallen those who had come before her.

Sarah's heart pounded as she heard distant, echoing screams. She wasn't alone in the caves. The realization sent a chill down her spine. Who or what else was trapped down here with her?

She pressed on, her eyes catching sight of strange symbols carved into the cave walls. They were similar to the ones she had seen around the campsite, only these were older, more weathered. The symbols seemed to pulse with a malevolent energy, making her skin crawl.

Turning a corner, Sarah was startled by the sight of another person. A young man, gaunt and pale, was huddled against the cave wall. He looked up at her with wide, terrified eyes. "Help me," he whispered, his voice hoarse and weak.

Sarah rushed to his side, helping him sit up. "My name is Sarah. How long have you been down here?"

"Days," he replied. "My name is Ethan. I was camping with some friends when we were attacked. The spirits... they dragged us down here. I think I'm the only one left."

Ethan told Sarah about the forest spirits and the blood rituals that sustained their power. He had stumbled upon an old journal in the cave that detailed the ancient practices used to bind the spirits and maintain the curse. Together, they decided to find a way out, using Ethan's knowledge of the cave system to navigate the labyrinthine passages.

Sarah and Ethan moved cautiously through the caves, the glow of the fungi casting eerie shadows on the walls. They encountered supernatural traps: pits that seemed to open up out of nowhere, and spectral figures that appeared and disappeared at will. But they pressed on, driven by the hope of escape.

After hours of navigating the treacherous terrain, they found a narrow passage leading upward. The faint light of the surface could be seen at the far end, offering a glimmer of hope. But their relief was short-lived. The path was guarded by the spirits, their forms flickering in and out of existence, eyes glowing with an otherworldly light.

A harrowing chase ensued. The spirits shrieked and wailed as they pursued Sarah and Ethan through the twisting tunnels. The ground seemed to shift beneath their feet, and the walls closed in, as if the cave itself were trying to trap them.

Just as they reached the exit, Ethan stopped and turned to face Sarah. There was a strange, sorrowful look in his eyes. "I'm sorry, Sarah," he said, his voice filled with regret. "I was part of the ritual. They needed a sacrifice, and I lured you here."

Sarah's blood ran cold. Before she could react, Ethan pushed past her, sprinting towards the light. The spirits surged forward, their wrath now fully focused on Sarah. She screamed, feeling their icy touch as they clawed at her, pulling her back into the darkness.

In a desperate last stand, Sarah grabbed a sharp piece of rock from the ground and fought back, slashing at the spirits with all her strength. But the odds were against her. The spirits were relentless, their shrieks filling the cavern as they closed in.

Her vision blurred, and she felt herself being dragged down. The last thing she saw was Ethan's silhouette disappearing into the light, leaving her to face the horrors alone. As the darkness enveloped her, she knew that the forest's ancient curse had claimed another victim, and the blood ritual would continue.

Chapter 3

The Ritual

Sarah's eyes fluttered open, her vision blurry and her head pounding. She tried to move, but her arms and legs were bound tightly to a tree. Panic surged through her as she realized she was back in the forest, surrounded by the spirits. They hovered around her, their translucent forms shimmering in the moonlight.

The clearing was marked with ancient symbols, carved into the trees and the ground. The air was thick with the scent of blood and decay, and the spirits chanted in a guttural language she couldn't understand. Their voices rose and fell in a hypnotic rhythm, preparing for a ritual she knew she wouldn't survive.

She struggled against her bonds, but they were too tight. The rough bark of the tree bit into her skin, and the cold air made her shiver uncontrollably. She had to find a way out before it was too late.

The spirits brought forward a blood-stained altar, placing it directly in front of Sarah. It was a crude slab of stone, slick with dark, congealed blood. One of the spirits, a towering figure with hollow eyes, stepped forward and began to cut into its own flesh with a jagged piece of obsidian.

As the blood flowed, the spirit marked Sarah's forehead and arms with dark, dripping symbols. She felt a dark power coursing through her veins, a malevolent force that sapped her strength and weakened her resolve. The chanting grew louder, more frenzied, as the spirits moved in closer, their eyes glowing with a terrifying intensity.

Sarah's mind raced. She couldn't let them complete the ritual. She had to find a way to stop them, to escape this nightmare.

Through the haze of pain and fear, Sarah spotted a group of hikers in the distance, moving through the forest. Hope surged within her. She screamed as loud as she could, trying to get their attention. The spirits momentarily paused, their heads turning towards the source of the noise.

The distraction was brief, but it was enough. With a burst of adrenaline, Sarah twisted her wrists and managed to slip one hand free from the ropes. She quickly worked on the other hand, ignoring the searing pain in her arms.

Once her hands were free, she untied her legs and bolted towards the hikers, her heart pounding in her chest. She ran as fast as she could, her breath coming in ragged gasps.

The spirits shrieked in fury and gave chase, their ghostly forms gliding through the trees with unnatural speed. Their cries echoed through the forest, a cacophony of rage and desperation. Sarah could hear them closing in, but she didn't dare look back.

She reached the hikers, who were startled by her sudden appearance. "We need to run! Now!" she screamed, grabbing one of them by the arm. They looked at her in confusion and fear, but the sight of the approaching spirits quickly convinced them of the danger.

The group sprinted through the dense woods, branches whipping against their faces and roots tripping their feet. The spirits were relentless, their howls growing louder and more insistent. The hikers, initially skeptical, soon realized the true danger as the spirits closed in, their forms becoming more solid and terrifying.

They reached a cliff, the ground dropping away into a dark abyss. There was nowhere left to run. Sarah turned to face the spirits, her back against the edge of the cliff. The hikers huddled behind her, their faces pale with fear.

"Stay behind me," Sarah said, her voice trembling but determined. She remembered what Ethan had told her about the spirits and the rituals. She had to confront them, to use their own power against them.

The spirits surged forward, their eyes glowing with malevolence. Sarah grabbed a sharp rock from the ground and carved a symbol into her palm, the pain sharp and immediate. She raised her hand, the blood dripping down her arm.

"In the name of the ancient ones, I command you to leave!" she shouted, her voice echoing through the forest. The spirits hesitated, their forms flickering. For a moment, it seemed like it might work.

But then the lead spirit lunged at her, its claws slashing through the air. Sarah fought back, swinging the rock with all her strength. The battle was brutal and bloody, the spirits' howls mixing with the hikers' screams.

Sarah felt their cold claws tearing at her flesh, but she didn't stop. She had to break the curse, to end the nightmare. With a final, desperate cry, she plunged the rock into the lead spirit's chest, carving the symbol deep into its ethereal form.

There was a blinding flash of light, and the spirits let out a collective scream. Their forms disintegrated, turning to smoke and ash that was carried away by the wind. The forest fell silent, the oppressive darkness lifting.

Sarah collapsed to the ground, her body bruised and bloodied. She had done it. The curse was broken. But as she lay there, staring up at the sky, she couldn't shake the feeling that the forest's ancient evil was still watching, waiting for its next victim.

Chapter 4

The Aftermath

Sarah and the hikers stumbled out of the forest, their bodies battered and their minds reeling from the horrors they had faced. The sun was beginning to rise, casting a pale light over the dense trees as they made their way down a narrow path that led to a nearby village.

The villagers, a small and tight-knit community, were wary of the newcomers. Whispers spread quickly as Sarah and the hikers sought help, their exhausted and bloodied appearances drawing concerned glances. They were given food and water, but the atmosphere was tense. The villagers spoke in hushed tones about the cursed forest and the legends that surrounded it.

As Sarah sat in the small village square, she couldn't shake the feeling of being watched. The forest loomed in the distance, a dark and foreboding presence that seemed to reach out with invisible tendrils.

Even after leaving the forest, Sarah couldn't escape its influence. Strange occurrences began to plague her. She saw shadows moving at the edge of her vision, heard whispers that seemed to come from nowhere, and felt an oppressive presence that made her skin crawl.

The hikers who had survived with her started to distance themselves. Fearful whispers spread among them, and they avoided her gaze. They believed the curse had followed them out of the forest, and their fear grew with each passing day.

Sarah felt isolated and desperate. She knew she had to find a way to end the curse once and for all. She couldn't live like this, and she couldn't let the darkness continue to spread.

Determined to find answers, Sarah sought out the local historian, an elderly woman named Agnes who was known for her knowledge of the village's history and the surrounding areas. Agnes welcomed her into her small, cluttered home, her eyes filled with a mix of curiosity and concern.

Sarah recounted her harrowing experience, and Agnes listened intently, nodding as if she had heard similar stories before. When Sarah finished, Agnes stood up and retrieved an old, leather-bound book from a dusty shelf.

"The forest has been cursed for centuries," Agnes explained, opening the book to a page filled with strange symbols and drawings. "The blood rituals were meant to bind and control the spirits, but something went wrong. The curse can be broken, but it requires a final ritual, one that is dangerous and difficult."

Sarah leaned forward, her heart pounding. "What do I need to do?"

Agnes detailed the steps of the ritual, which involved returning to the heart of the forest and using specific symbols and incantations to banish the spirits once and for all. The ritual required great courage and resolve, as the spirits would do everything in their power to stop it.

Sarah faced a difficult decision. She could risk her life to end the curse or live in constant fear, haunted by the darkness that followed her. She knew what she had to do.

"I'm going back," she said, her voice steady. "I have to finish this."

Agnes nodded and handed her the ancient book. "Be careful, Sarah. The forest won't let you go easily."

Sarah entered the forest alone, her heart pounding with a mix of fear and determination. The trees seemed to close in around her, their branches reaching out like skeletal fingers. The air was thick with an oppressive energy, and the whispers grew louder with each step she took.

She reached the clearing where the initial ritual had taken place. The blood-stained altar was still there, a grim reminder of what had happened. Sarah opened the book and began to prepare for the final ritual, drawing the necessary symbols on the ground and chanting the ancient incantations.

As she started the ritual, the spirits appeared, their forms flickering in and out of existence. They shrieked in fury, their eyes glowing with a malevolent light. Sarah's hands trembled, but she continued the ritual, determined to see it through.

The spirits attacked, their icy claws slashing at her skin. Blood flowed freely, and Sarah screamed in pain, but she didn't stop. She fought back, using the symbols and incantations to fend off their attacks.

The forest seemed to come alive with their fury, the ground shaking and the trees swaying violently. Sarah's vision blurred, but she kept going, drawing on every ounce of strength she had left.

With a final, desperate cry, she completed the ritual. The spirits let out a collective scream, their forms disintegrating into smoke and ash. The oppressive energy lifted, and the forest fell silent.

Sarah collapsed to the ground, her body bruised and bloodied. She had done it. The curse was broken. But as she lay there, staring up at the sky, she couldn't shake the feeling that something dark still lingered in the depths of the forest, waiting for its next victim.

Chapter 5

The Final Truth

Sarah lay in a small bed in the village clinic, her body wrapped in bandages and her mind reeling from the events of the past days. Villagers had found her unconscious at the edge of the forest and brought her back, tending to her wounds. She was weak, but alive, and for the first time, she allowed herself to believe that the nightmare was over.

The villagers praised her bravery, whispering that she had broken the curse that had plagued their community for generations. Sarah nodded and accepted their gratitude, but a nagging feeling of unease lingered in the back of her mind. She couldn't shake the memories of the forest and the spirits, nor the sense that something was still wrong.

As she lay there, she reflected on her ordeal. She had faced unimaginable horrors and survived. But at what cost? The uneasy peace that had settled over her did little to quell the growing dread in her heart.

Days turned into weeks, and Sarah slowly began to rebuild her life. She tried to dismiss the strange occurrences that continued to plague her: shadows that moved on their own, whispers that seemed to come from nowhere, and the feeling of being watched. She told herself it was just the remnants of her trauma, lingering fears that would eventually fade.

But the nightmares were relentless. Every night, she dreamt of the forest, of dark shadows and whispering voices that called out to her. She would wake up drenched in sweat, her heart pounding, and the sense of dread growing stronger with each passing night.

Despite her efforts to move on, the forest's grip on her mind remained tight. She began to wonder if she had truly broken the curse or merely delayed the inevitable. One evening, Agnes visited Sarah with a look of grave concern. She held the old, leather-bound book tightly, her knuckles white.

"Sarah, I fear the ritual you performed was incomplete," Agnes said, her voice trembling. "The last pages of the book, the ones containing the critical steps, were torn out. I didn't realize it until now."

Sarah's blood ran cold. "What does that mean?"

"It means the curse was not broken. The spirits were not banished. They were merely awakened, and they're growing stronger."

Panic surged through Sarah as she realized the true horror hadn't ended. The unease she had felt was the curse tightening its grip on her. She knew she had to act quickly to find the missing pages and complete the ritual properly.

Driven by desperation, Sarah returned to the forest. The villagers begged her not to go, fearing for her safety, but she couldn't stay. She had to end this once and for all.

The forest seemed darker and more hostile than before. The shadows were deeper, the whispers louder. She made her way to the clearing where the rituals had taken place, her heart pounding in her chest.

As she searched, she discovered something that chilled her to the bone: Ethan's betrayal was part of a larger, darker plan. He had been a pawn of the spirits, used to bring Sarah to the forest and ensure the ritual would awaken their true master.

The spirits revealed themselves, their forms more solid and menacing than before. They surrounded her, their eyes glowing with malevolent intent. But this time, they did not attack. Instead, they led her deeper into the forest, to a place she had never seen before.

In the heart of the forest, Sarah faced an ancient, powerful entity. Its form was a swirling mass of shadows and dark energy, its eyes burning with a hellish light. The spirits bowed before it, their master.

The entity spoke in a voice that shook the very ground beneath her feet. "You have done well, Sarah. You have awakened me. Now, complete the ritual and unleash my power fully."

Sarah's mind raced as she realized the depth of her mistake. The final ritual wasn't meant to break the curse; it was meant to release the entity's full power. She had been a pawn in its game, and now she was the key to its freedom.

Desperate, she tried to resist, but the entity's power was overwhelming. It forced her to recite the incantations, her voice echoing through the forest as the ritual progressed. She felt her will being stripped away, her body moving against her control.

With the final words, the ground shook violently, and the forest was bathed in a blinding light. The entity let out a triumphant roar as its power was fully unleashed. Sarah collapsed to the ground, her mind and body broken.

As she lay there, the entity began its reign of terror, spreading darkness and fear. The villagers screamed as the forest came alive with malevolent spirits, and the ancient curse consumed everything in its path.

Sarah's last thought was a chilling realization: the true horror had just begun, and there was no escape from the Blood Forest.

The Abyss Below

Chapter 1

The Descent

The remote cave system nestled in the mountains had long been a subject of fascination for geologists and adventurers alike. Lisa, a dedicated geologist, had assembled a small team to explore its depths. Alongside her were Tom, an experienced caver with countless expeditions under his belt, and Alex, a biologist eager to discover new subterranean life forms.

The three stood at the cave entrance, a yawning maw in the mountainside that seemed to beckon them into darkness. The air was cool and damp, carrying the earthy scent of untouched depths. Their excitement was palpable as they checked their equipment one last time before descending into the abyss.

"Ready?" Lisa asked, her voice echoing slightly in the cavernous space. Tom and Alex nodded, and with a shared look of determination, they stepped into the darkness.

As they descended deeper into the cave, their headlamps illuminated the stunning beauty of the underground world. Stalactites hung like chandeliers from the ceiling, and the walls were adorned with glittering mineral deposits. The atmosphere was almost serene, but as they moved further in, the cave began to reveal its more sinister side.

Strange markings appeared on the walls, resembling ancient symbols or hieroglyphs. Alex ran his fingers over them, frowning. "These don't look like natural formations," he muttered. "Almost like they were carved by someone—or something."

A sense of unease settled over the group. Lisa tried to shake it off, focusing on the geological wonders around her, but the further they went, the stronger the feeling grew.

Deeper into the cave, the team stumbled upon a gruesome discovery. Piles of bones, some clearly animal and some disturbingly human, littered the ground. Some of the bones looked fresh, with remnants of flesh still clinging to them.

"Something's not right," Tom said, his voice tight with concern. "We need to be careful."

The cave opened into a vast, dark chamber that seemed to swallow their light. The air was thick and heavy, making it difficult to breathe. Lisa spotted a narrow passageway hidden behind a curtain of stalactites. "Over here," she called, her voice barely above a whisper.

The passage beckoned them deeper into the unknown, and despite their growing apprehension, they couldn't resist the urge to explore further.

As they ventured down the narrow passage, the atmosphere grew more oppressive. Strange noises echoed around them—scratching, shuffling, and an occasional low growl that set their nerves on edge. The walls seemed to close in, and the air grew colder with each step.

Without warning, a shadowy figure lunged at Tom from the darkness. He cried out as claws raked across his chest, leaving deep, bloody gashes. The creature vanished as quickly as it had appeared, leaving Tom gasping in pain.

"We need to get out of here!" Lisa shouted, her voice echoing in the narrow space. The realization that they were not alone, that something was hunting them, sent a wave of panic through the group.

Their retreat was frantic. Every shadow seemed to move, every sound amplified by their fear. As they retraced their steps, the oppressive presence grew stronger. The feeling of being watched was unbearable.

Then, from the darkness, the monster revealed itself. A towering creature with glowing, malevolent eyes and razor-sharp claws. Its body was a mass of sinew and muscle, covered in dark, matted fur. It let out a guttural roar that shook the very walls of the cave.

A bloody chase ensued. The team sprinted through the twisting passages, the creature hot on their heels. Its claws scraped against the stone, and its roars echoed in their ears. They could feel its hot breath on their necks as they ran for their lives.

They reached a dead end, a sheer rock face blocking their path. Panic set in as they turned to face the approaching horror. The monster slowed, savoring its prey. Its eyes glowed with a predatory gleam, and it bared its teeth in a sinister grin.

Lisa, Tom, and Alex stood back to back, weapons at the ready, knowing they were in a fight for their lives against an ancient, unstoppable terror.

Chapter 2

The Abyss Strikes

Lisa, Tom, and Alex stood cornered, the monstrous creature advancing towards them with deliberate, predatory steps. Its eyes glowed with an unholy light, and its claws dripped with Tom's blood. The oppressive darkness of the cave seemed to close in around them, amplifying their terror.

"Use your equipment!" Lisa shouted, her voice barely audible over the creature's growls. Tom, despite his injuries, brandished a climbing pick, while Alex held a flare gun with trembling hands.

The monster lunged. Tom swung his pick, the metal embedding in the creature's thick hide. It roared in pain and fury, swiping at Tom with its claws. Alex fired the flare gun, the bright light temporarily blinding the beast and causing it to recoil.

"Run!" Lisa screamed, and they bolted down a narrow passage, the monster's roars echoing behind them. They had injured it, but not stopped it. The chase was far from over.

They moved deeper into the cave, their breaths coming in ragged gasps. The cave seemed to twist and shift around them, as if it were alive, conspiring to trap them within its depths. The walls pulsed with a malevolent energy, and the ground beneath their feet felt unstable.

The monster's roars echoed through the passages, a constant reminder of the danger that stalked them. Every sound seemed amplified, every shadow a potential threat. The oppressive darkness pressed in on them, making it difficult to see or think clearly.

"There's no way out," Tom muttered, his voice tinged with despair. "We're trapped."

"We have to keep moving," Lisa said, trying to sound more confident than she felt. "There has to be another exit."

But as they pressed on, the cave itself seemed to turn against them. Passages that should have led to safety twisted back on themselves, leading them in circles. The walls closed in, and the air grew colder, as if the cave was a living entity, determined to consume them.

As they ventured further, Alex began to show signs of psychological distress. He would stop suddenly, staring into the darkness with wide, fearful eyes. "Do you hear that?" he whispered. "Voices... they're calling my name."

Lisa tried to reassure him, but the pressure was mounting. The darkness played tricks on their minds, and the constant fear of the monster's return gnawed at their sanity.

"We need to stay together," Lisa said firmly, though her own resolve was weakening. "We can't afford to lose our heads."

They stumbled upon a deep chasm, its depths lost to darkness. With no other options, they decided to descend, hoping it might lead to an exit. The climb down was treacherous, the walls slick with moisture and loose rocks.

At the bottom of the chasm, they found themselves in the monster's lair. The air was thick with the stench of decay, and the ground was littered with bones and rotting flesh. The walls were slick with blood, and strange symbols were etched into the stone, glowing faintly with an eerie light.

Lisa gagged at the smell, covering her mouth with her hand. "This is its feeding ground," she whispered. "We're in its territory now."

They found remnants of past victims—clothing, personal items, and notes scrawled in desperation. Among the remains, they found evidence that the monster was ancient, possibly immortal. Drawings and carvings depicted the creature hunting and feeding, stretching back centuries.

Their horror was compounded by the realization that they were not the first to fall prey to the monster, and they would not be the last.

The monster's return was heralded by a bone-chilling roar that echoed through the lair. It emerged from the shadows, more enraged and terrifying than before. Its eyes burned with an insatiable hunger, and its claws gleamed with deadly intent.

"Get ready!" Lisa shouted, her voice trembling. Tom, weakened by his injuries, struggled to lift his pick. Alex brandished a makeshift weapon, his hands shaking.

The monster attacked with ferocious speed. Tom swung his pick, but the creature swatted him aside like a rag doll. He hit the ground hard, blood pouring from his wounds. Alex thrust his weapon at the beast, but it barely slowed it down.

In the chaos, Lisa grabbed Alex's arm. "We have to go, now!"

Tom, gasping for breath, managed a weak smile. "Go... I'll hold it off."

Tears streamed down Lisa's face as she pulled Alex away. "I'm sorry," she whispered.

They ran, leaving Tom behind as the monster descended upon him. His screams echoed through the cave, mingling with the creature's triumphant roars. The sound of tearing flesh and crunching bones followed them as they fled deeper into the darkness.

Lisa and Alex stumbled through the twisting passages, their hearts pounding with fear and grief. The cave seemed to close in around them, and the monster's presence loomed ever closer, an unstoppable force of nature that would not rest until it had claimed them all.

Chapter 3

The Depths of Despair

Lisa and Alex stumbled through the dark, twisting passages, their breaths coming in ragged gasps. The monster's roars echoed behind them, a constant reminder of the terror that pursued them. The cave seemed to stretch on endlessly, each turn and corridor blending into the next, trapping them in a nightmarish labyrinth.

As they moved deeper, they stumbled upon more remnants of previous victims: shattered bones, torn clothing, and discarded personal items. Each discovery increased their dread, a grim reminder of the fate that awaited them if they couldn't find a way out.

The cave seemed to taunt them. Shadows shifted just beyond the reach of their lights, and whispers grew louder, carrying words they couldn't understand but felt deep in their bones. The air was thick with an oppressive energy, making it hard to breathe.

They came upon an old, forgotten tunnel, partially hidden by fallen rocks and debris. The entrance was narrow, and the air that wafted from it was cold and stale. Desperation drove them forward, hoping this tunnel might lead them away from the relentless monster.

The tunnel walls were lined with ancient, blood-stained handprints, a macabre trail left by those who had come before them. As they ventured further, the temperature dropped, and the air grew heavier. They could hear distant cries, echoes of the monster's past victims, their agony reverberating through the stone.

Every step felt like a march toward their doom, but they had no other choice. The monster's roars echoed closer, pushing them onward.

The tunnel opened into a massive cavern, filled with towering stalagmites and eerie, glowing crystals embedded in the walls. The light from the crystals cast long, shifting shadows that danced menacingly around them. The cavern amplified every sound, making it hard to distinguish between real and imagined threats.

Lisa and Alex moved cautiously, their senses on high alert. They heard footsteps and breathing, but couldn't tell where they were coming from. Every noise echoed, creating a disorienting cacophony that frayed their nerves.

"We need to stay together," Lisa whispered, her voice barely audible over the din.

Alex nodded, his face pale with fear. "What if... what if it's playing with us?"

Lisa didn't answer. She didn't want to admit that the thought had crossed her mind too.

As they navigated the cavern, they stumbled upon a disturbing sight: a shrine made of bones and tattered clothing. The bones were arranged in intricate patterns, and the clothing bore the stains of blood and decay. The shrine seemed to pulsate with a dark energy, radiating malevolence.

Lisa's stomach churned. "It's a trap," she whispered. "The monster set this up."

Before they could react, the monster struck. It emerged from the shadows, its glowing eyes filled with sadistic glee. It lunged at Alex, its claws raking across his side, sending him sprawling to the ground with a scream.

Lisa grabbed a rock and threw it at the creature, trying to distract it. "Over here!" she shouted, her voice trembling with fear. The monster turned its attention to her, its gaze piercing through her soul.

With Alex gravely wounded, Lisa knew they had to act fast. She helped him to his feet, and they hobbled toward a cluster of the glowing crystals. The crystals emitted a strange, pulsating light that seemed to repel the monster, if only slightly.

"We can use these," Lisa said, her voice filled with desperation. "We can create a barrier."

They quickly arranged the crystals in a circle, hoping to hold the monster at bay. The creature roared in frustration, circling the barrier, its eyes never leaving them.

"We can't stay here forever," Alex said, his voice weak from pain. "What are we going to do?"

Lisa took a deep breath, her mind racing. "I'm going to distract it. You have to find a way out."

Alex's eyes widened. "No, you can't—"

"It's the only way," Lisa insisted. "You need to survive."

With a final, determined look, Lisa stepped outside the barrier, holding one of the crystals in front of her like a shield. The monster lunged at her, and she threw the crystal with all her strength, shattering it against the creature's hide.

The monster howled in pain, but it only seemed to enrage it further. It turned on Lisa, its claws slashing through the air. She dodged and weaved, trying to stay ahead of its attacks, but it was relentless.

"Go, Alex! Now!" she screamed, her voice echoing through the cavern.

Alex hesitated for a moment, tears streaming down his face, before turning and limping toward the tunnel. Lisa fought with every ounce of strength she had, but she knew it was only a matter of time.

The monster broke through the makeshift barrier, its eyes gleaming with triumph. It lunged at Lisa, and she felt its claws sink into her flesh. Pain exploded through her body, and she fell to the ground, her vision fading.

As darkness closed in, her last thought was of Alex, and the hope that he would find a way out of the cave. The monster's roar echoed through the cavern, a chilling reminder that the abyss had claimed another victim.

Chapter 4

The Descent into Hell

Alex limped through the dark tunnels, his heart pounding and his breath coming in ragged gasps. Lisa's screams echoed behind him, a haunting reminder of the sacrifice she had made. The cave seemed to stretch on forever, a never-ending maze of shadows and despair.

The air grew colder, each breath a painful struggle. His vision blurred, and the walls of the cave seemed to pulse with a malevolent energy. He could hear the monster's roars growing fainter, a small glimmer of hope in the overwhelming darkness. Maybe, just maybe, he could escape.

As he pushed forward, the cave began to play tricks on his mind. Vivid hallucinations assailed him, visions of Lisa appearing in the shadows. She was bloodied and broken, her eyes wide with fear and desperation.

"Help me, Alex," she whispered, her voice echoing in his ears. "Don't leave me here."

He shook his head, trying to clear the images, but they only grew stronger. The cave walls seemed to close in on him, the passageway narrowing and twisting. He stumbled, his hands scraping against the rough stone as he fought to distinguish reality from illusion.

The whispers grew louder, filling his mind with doubts and fears. He could hear voices, some familiar and others foreign, all urging him to give in, to let the darkness take him.

In his delirium, Alex stumbled upon a vast, seemingly bottomless pit within the cave. The air around it was thick with a choking, sulfuric scent, and the edges of the pit were jagged and crumbling. He peered into the abyss, the darkness so complete it seemed to swallow all light.

Whispering voices rose from the depths, insidious and compelling. They promised an end to his suffering, a release from the terror that consumed him. The ground around the pit was littered with bones, the remnants of those who had succumbed to the whispers.

Alex teetered on the edge, his mind battling against the seductive call of the abyss. He could feel the pull, the promise of peace, but something deep within him refused to give in.

Just as he regained some semblance of sanity, the monster reappeared. It emerged from the shadows, more grotesque and terrifying than before. Its body was covered in fresh wounds, blood oozing from the gashes. Its eyes burned with a vengeful fury, and its roars echoed through the cave, causing rocks and debris to fall from the ceiling.

The ground shook with each step it took, and Alex's heart raced with fear. The monster advanced, its claws gleaming in the dim light. The cave seemed to shrink around him, trapping him in a nightmare with no escape.

Alex found himself cornered, the bottomless pit behind him and the monster advancing. Desperation surged through him, and he grabbed a loose rock, wielding it as a makeshift weapon. He swung it at the creature, but it barely slowed it down.

The monster lunged, its claws raking across Alex's chest, tearing through flesh and bone. He screamed in pain, but adrenaline kept him moving. He fought with every ounce of strength he had left, using the rock to strike at the monster's head.

In a desperate move, Alex lunged at the monster, trying to push it into the pit. The creature roared, its claws sinking into his flesh as they teetered on the edge. The ground crumbled beneath their weight, and with a final, blood-curdling scream, they both plunged into the abyss.

The darkness enveloped them, the whispers growing louder as they fell. Alex's last thought was of Lisa, and the hope that she had somehow escaped the horrors of the cave.

The pit swallowed them whole, the silence returning as the echoes of their struggle faded into nothingness. The cave remained, a silent, malevolent presence, waiting for its next victims.

Chapter 5

The Eternal Darkness

Alex plunged into the abyss, the darkness swallowing him whole. His screams echoed as he fell, but the void absorbed the sound, leaving only silence. He hit the ground hard, pain exploding through his body. Gasping for breath, he realized he had landed in a subterranean chamber, deep beneath the cave.

The atmosphere was thick and oppressive, the air heavy with the scent of decay. Faint, eerie whispers surrounded him, seeming to come from the very walls themselves. Alex struggled to move, his body battered and bruised from the fall.

As he crawled through the chamber, his hands brushed against bones and fragments of clothing. The remnants of past victims littered the ground, their final moments frozen in silent agony. Alex's heart pounded with fear as he took in the horrific scene.

Among the debris, he found a tattered journal, its pages yellowed with age. With trembling hands, he opened it and began to read. The journal belonged to a previous explorer, who had detailed the existence of an ancient, malevolent entity that dwelled within the cave. This entity fed on fear and despair, using a monstrous servant to capture and torment its victims.

The more Alex read, the more he understood the true horror of his situation. The monster was merely a tool, a harbinger of the greater evil that lurked in the shadows.

As he continued to read, Alex felt an ominous presence watching him. The whispers grew louder, and the ground beneath him began to tremble. A shadowy form started to materialize in the center of the chamber, coalescing into a monstrous amalgamation of darkness and eyes.

The entity had awakened.

Its many eyes stared at Alex, each one filled with malice and hunger. The air crackled with dark energy, and Alex's fear intensified, feeding the entity's power.

Desperate to escape, Alex tried to find a way out of the chamber, but the entity's power warped reality around him. He stumbled through twisted corridors that seemed to change with each step, encountering nightmarish visions of his past. Memories twisted into grotesque versions of themselves, each more terrifying than the last.

The entity toyed with his mind, breaking his will. He saw visions of his loved ones, their faces contorted in pain and suffering. The whispers grew louder, turning into screams that echoed in his head.

"There's no escape," the entity's voice boomed, a sound that seemed to come from everywhere and nowhere. "You belong to me now."

In a final, desperate moment, Alex saw Lisa standing before him. She looked unharmed, her eyes filled with hope. "Alex, it's me! We can escape together," she said, reaching out to him.

For a moment, hope flared within him. He reached for her hand, but as their fingers touched, her form shimmered and distorted. She smiled, her eyes turning dark. "Did you really think you could escape?" she whispered, her voice morphing into the entity's.

The realization hit Alex like a blow. Lisa was an illusion, a cruel trick played by the entity to break his spirit. The chamber darkened, and the true horror of his situation became clear.

The entity revealed the final, horrifying truth: Alex had never left the cave. From the moment he and his team entered, they had been trapped in its nightmarish grip. It had been feeding on their fear, using their memories and emotions to sustain itself.

The monster reappeared, its eyes glowing with triumph. It lunged at Alex, and he felt its claws sink into his flesh. Pain and darkness enveloped him, and his screams were swallowed by the abyss.

As the entity consumed him, Alex's soul was trapped forever in its realm, a prisoner of the eternal darkness. The cave remained, silent and malevolent, waiting for its next victims to wander into its depths.

Carnival of Terror

Chapter 1

The Abandoned Carnival

The abandoned carnival stood on the outskirts of town, a relic of happier times now shrouded in decay and mystery. Jenna, always the thrill-seeker, had convinced her boyfriend Mike and their cautious friend Sarah to explore it with her. They arrived at dusk, the setting sun casting long shadows over the rusted rides and broken attractions.

"Are you sure this is a good idea?" Sarah asked, her voice tinged with anxiety.

"It'll be fun," Jenna replied, her eyes gleaming with excitement. "It's just an old carnival. What's the worst that could happen?"

Mike shrugged, trying to appear nonchalant, but even he felt a knot of unease in his stomach. Together, they pushed open the creaking gate and stepped into the carnival grounds.

The entrance was eerily intact, with faded colors and cracked paint giving it a ghostly appearance. Broken rides loomed in the distance, their once-vibrant hues now dulled by time. The atmosphere was unsettling, and the faint sound of carnival music played somewhere in the background, a haunting melody that seemed to come from nowhere.

"Let's check out the funhouse first," Jenna suggested, leading the way. Mike and Sarah exchanged wary glances but followed her nonetheless.

As they moved deeper into the carnival, the sense of dread grew stronger. They passed creepy clown statues, their painted smiles cracked and peeling, and old posters advertising long-forgotten shows. The air was thick with the scent of rust and decay.

They soon found themselves at the entrance of the funhouse, its garish facade a stark contrast to the surrounding gloom. The door creaked open as Jenna pushed it, and they stepped inside. The interior was dark, lit only by flickering bulbs that cast eerie shadows on the walls.

"This place gives me the creeps," Mike muttered, glancing around nervously.

"Don't be such a baby," Jenna teased, but even she felt a shiver run down her spine.

As they moved through the funhouse, they experienced strange and disturbing illusions. The mirrors distorted their reflections, making them appear grotesque and monstrous. They heard footsteps and distant laughter, but each time they turned around, there was no one there.

In the maze of mirrors, they became separated. Jenna wandered alone, her reflection multiplying around her. She saw a figure in the distance, its form distorted by the mirrors. As it drew closer, she realized with horror that it was a clown—a sinister figure with sharp teeth and bloodstained clothes.

The clown grinned, its eyes glinting with malice. Jenna screamed as it lunged at her, slashing her arm with a blade. Blood spattered the mirrors, and she stumbled back, clutching her wound. The clown laughed, a chilling sound that echoed through the funhouse, before disappearing into the shadows.

Jenna managed to find Mike and Sarah, her face pale and her arm bleeding profusely. "We need to get out of here," she gasped, her voice trembling with fear.

They hurried towards the exit, but the funhouse seemed to conspire against them. The corridors twisted and turned, leading them in circles. The exits they found were blocked, and the clown's laughter echoed around them, growing louder and more menacing.

"Over here!" Mike shouted, spotting a possible way out. But as they ran towards it, the clown appeared, blocking their path. It loomed over them, its teeth bared in a grotesque smile, its eyes filled with hunger.

Trapped and terrified, they realized there was no escape. The clown advanced, its intentions clear and deadly, and they knew they were about to become the next victims of the Carnival of Terror.

Chapter 2

The Clown's Lair

The clown's grotesque smile widened as it advanced on them, its razor-sharp teeth gleaming in the dim light. Jenna, Mike, and Sarah scrambled to find anything they could use as a weapon. Mike grabbed a broken piece of wood, while Sarah found a rusty metal pipe. Jenna, clutching her bleeding arm, picked up a shard of glass.

The clown lunged at them, its laughter echoing through the funhouse. They fought desperately, striking at the clown with their makeshift weapons. Each blow seemed to have little effect, the clown's maniacal laughter growing louder with each strike.

With a stroke of luck, Mike managed to land a hit on the clown's head, causing it to stagger back. "Run!" he shouted, and they bolted, leaving the injured clown behind. Jenna's wound was getting worse, and she struggled to keep up, her vision blurring from the pain and blood loss.

They fled deeper into the carnival, the eerie music and unsettling atmosphere growing more oppressive. Animatronics, long broken and decayed, seemed to come to life, their eyes following the trio as they passed. Ghostly whispers filled the air, and shadows danced at the edges of their vision, making it hard to distinguish what was real.

"Where do we go?" Sarah panted, fear etched into her face.

"There!" Jenna pointed to an old maintenance shed, its door slightly ajar. They rushed inside, slamming the door shut behind them. The small room was cluttered with old tools and equipment, the air thick with dust and decay.

Inside the shed, they discovered old newspaper clippings and photographs pinned to the walls. The headlines told a grim story: "Carnival Performer Goes Mad," "Clown's Killing Spree Shocks Town," "Missing Persons Linked to Carnival."

Jenna picked up a faded photograph of the clown in happier times, surrounded by children. "He was a performer here," she whispered, her voice trembling. "He went mad and started killing people."

The shed was filled with disturbing remnants of the clown's past victims—torn clothing, personal items, and splatters of dried blood. The realization that they were dealing with a deranged, supernatural killer sank in, and the horror of their situation deepened.

A loud crash jolted them out of their thoughts. The clown had found them, bursting through the shed door with renewed fury. It attacked with a ferocity they hadn't seen before, its eyes blazing with a murderous rage.

They fought back desperately, but the clown seemed almost invulnerable, shrugging off their attacks as if they were nothing. In the chaos, the clown grabbed Mike, its claws digging into his flesh. "No!" Jenna screamed, but it was too late. The clown dragged Mike away, his screams echoing through the darkness.

Jenna and Sarah fled from the shed, Mike's anguished cries haunting their every step. They ran blindly through the carnival, pursued by the relentless clown. The haunted house attraction loomed before them, its entrance a gaping maw of darkness. They had no choice but to enter.

Inside, the attraction was a nightmare come to life. Animatronics of twisted clowns and grotesque figures lunged at them, their mechanical movements jerky and unsettling. Illusions of blood and gore filled the air, creating a disorienting and terrifying environment.

"Keep going!" Jenna urged, her voice barely audible over the cacophony of screams and laughter.

They stumbled through the haunted house, the clown's footsteps growing louder behind them. Just when they thought they were trapped, Sarah spotted a hidden door in the floor. They pried it open and found a narrow underground tunnel.

"This is our only chance," Sarah said, her voice shaking. They climbed down into the tunnel, the darkness swallowing them as they descended. The sound of the clown's laughter echoed above them, a chilling reminder that their ordeal was far from over.

Chapter 3

The Tunnel of Nightmares

Jenna and Sarah crawled through the narrow, claustrophobic tunnel, the darkness pressing in on them from all sides. The air was thick with dampness, making it difficult to breathe. Their hands and knees scraped against the rough stone floor, and the distant, eerie laughter of the clown echoed through the tunnel, growing louder with each passing moment.

The tunnel walls were covered in strange, unsettling graffiti. Crude drawings of the clown, alongside warnings like "Beware the Clown" and "Turn Back Now," seemed to glow faintly in the darkness. The unsettling imagery heightened their sense of dread, and they couldn't shake the feeling that they were being watched.

As they moved deeper into the tunnel, they stumbled upon alcoves carved into the walls. Each alcove contained mummified remains of past victims, their bodies posed in lifelike positions as if frozen in their final moments of terror. Some appeared to be screaming, while others reached out with skeletal hands, pleading for help that never came.

Jenna and Sarah's hearts pounded as they realized they were walking through the clown's macabre gallery. The sight of the preserved corpses filled them with a profound horror, the realization of the true extent of the clown's madness sinking in.

The tunnel began to narrow, forcing them to crawl on their hands and knees. The confined space made every movement difficult, and the sound of their own breathing seemed amplified in the suffocating darkness.

Behind them, the clown's laughter turned into growls and snarls, a menacing reminder of the danger that pursued them. Panic set in as Jenna felt the tunnel walls closing in around her, her body momentarily stuck. She struggled to free herself, the sound of the clown growing closer.

"Jenna, hurry!" Sarah whispered urgently, her voice trembling with fear. Jenna managed to pull herself free, her heart racing as they continued their desperate crawl through the tunnel.

They emerged into a larger chamber, filled with distorted funhouse mirrors. The mirrors reflected their worst fears, creating nightmarish illusions that seemed to leap out at them. Jenna saw her own reflection twisted and grotesque, her face contorted with terror. Sarah's reflection showed her covered in blood, with the lifeless eyes of the clown staring back at her.

The clown appeared in the reflections, its sinister grin taunting them from every angle. "You can't escape," it whispered, its voice echoing through the chamber. "You're mine."

The distorted images and the clown's presence made it difficult to distinguish reality from illusion. Jenna and Sarah clung to each other, their minds struggling to comprehend the horrors before them.

Desperate to escape the hallucinatory nightmare, they found a hidden passage leading to the clown's lair. The lair was a grotesque throne room, filled with trophies of its victims—bones, tattered clothing, and gruesome mementos. The air was thick with the stench of death and decay.

The clown lunged at them from the shadows, its eyes gleaming with sadistic pleasure. Jenna and Sarah fought back with anything they could find—rusty tools, broken pieces of wood, and shards of glass. The brutal fight ensued, their screams echoing through the lair as they struggled for their lives.

In the chaos, the clown slashed at Sarah with its razor-sharp claws, leaving deep, bloody wounds. She collapsed to the ground, gasping for breath as blood pooled around her. Jenna, filled with rage and desperation, continued to fight, but the clown's strength was overwhelming.

The chapter ended with Jenna facing the clown alone, her eyes filled with determination and fear. The clown's sinister laughter filled the lair, promising a gruesome end to their nightmare.

Chapter 4

The Final Showdown

Jenna stood alone in the lair, the air thick with the stench of decay and the oppressive presence of the clown. The sinister figure emerged from the shadows, its grotesque face twisted into a mocking grin. Bloodstains marked its clothes, remnants of countless victims who had fallen prey to its sadistic games.

"Welcome to the grand finale," the clown taunted, its voice a chilling whisper that seemed to come from all directions. "Do you like my collection?"

Jenna's eyes darted around the room, taking in the macabre displays of bones and tattered clothing. Her heart pounded, but her resolve hardened. She couldn't let fear control her. She had to fight, not just for herself, but for Sarah.

"I'm not afraid of you," Jenna said, her voice steady despite the terror gripping her heart. "Let's finish this."

The clown's grin widened, revealing rows of sharp, bloodstained teeth. "Very well," it said. With a snap of its fingers, the room around them began to shift and warp, the walls closing in and the floor transforming into a treacherous landscape of pitfalls and spikes.

Jenna dodged and weaved, narrowly avoiding several deadly traps. Razor-sharp blades swung from the ceiling, and hidden pits opened up beneath her feet. The clown's laughter echoed around her, growing louder with each close call.

"Isn't this fun?" the clown cackled, its voice bouncing off the walls in a disorienting cacophony. Jenna's fear threatened to overwhelm her, but she forced herself to stay focused. She couldn't afford to make a single mistake.

Suddenly, the clown appeared before her, its eyes gleaming with malicious glee. "Let's play a game," it hissed. "If you win, you and your friend can go free. If you lose... well, you'll join my collection."

Jenna's heart sank. She had no choice. "What's the game?" she asked, her voice barely more than a whisper.

The clown gestured to a twisted maze that had materialized in the center of the lair. "Navigate the maze," it said. "Reach the center, and you'll find your friend. Fail, and you'll die."

Jenna nodded, steeling herself for the challenge ahead. She had to save Sarah. She couldn't let the clown win.

Jenna entered the maze, the walls closing behind her. The air was thick with a putrid stench, and the flickering lights cast eerie shadows that seemed to move on their own. Grotesque animatronics lunged at her from hidden alcoves, their twisted faces contorted in eternal screams.

As she navigated the maze, Jenna encountered visions of her friends and family, their faces twisted into horrifying masks of pain and fear. She knew they weren't real, but the sight of them nearly broke her resolve. The clown appeared intermittently, attacking her with brutal force before vanishing into the shadows.

Jenna fought back with everything she had, using her wits and strength to overcome each obstacle. She was covered in cuts and bruises, her body aching with exhaustion, but she refused to give up.

Finally, Jenna reached the center of the maze, where the clown awaited on a bloodstained stage. The air was thick with the scent of blood, and the floor was slick with gore. Jenna's heart pounded as she faced her enemy, knowing this was her final chance.

The battle was brutal and bloody. The clown lunged at her with terrifying speed, its claws raking across her skin. Jenna fought back with all her strength, using the environment to her advantage. She grabbed a broken piece of wood and swung it at the clown, the sharp edge cutting into its flesh.

The clown roared in pain, its eyes burning with fury. Jenna pressed her advantage, striking again and again, each blow fueled by her determination to survive. Finally, in a climactic moment, she managed to fatally wound the clown, driving the wood deep into its chest.

The clown let out a final, ear-piercing scream before collapsing to the ground, its body convulsing as blood pooled around it. Jenna stood over it, breathing heavily, her body trembling with exhaustion and adrenaline.

She stumbled forward, finding Sarah barely alive, lying in a corner of the maze. "Sarah," Jenna whispered, tears streaming down her face. "We have to go."

Together, they struggled to their feet, supporting each other as they made their way out of the collapsing lair. The walls shook and the ground trembled, but they refused to stop. They had survived the nightmare, but the scars would remain forever.

As they emerged into the night, the carnival behind them crumbled into ruins. The clown was dead, but its sinister laughter echoed in their minds, a haunting reminder of the horrors they had faced.

Chapter 5

The Clown's Curse

Jenna and Sarah stumbled out of the carnival grounds, their bodies battered and minds reeling from the horrors they had faced. The night air was cool and quiet, a stark contrast to the nightmare they had just escaped. They found a deserted road and began walking, hoping to find help.

"We did it," Sarah whispered, trying to convince herself. "We're safe now."

But the eerie silence of the night was broken only by their labored breathing, and a sense of unease still lingered.

As they walked, the sound of faint footsteps echoed behind them. They turned around, seeing nothing but darkness. The feeling of being watched grew stronger, and their dread intensified.

"Do you hear that?" Jenna asked, her voice trembling.

Sarah nodded, gripping Jenna's arm tighter. "We need to keep moving."

Jenna's injuries worsened, her steps faltering. Each movement sent waves of pain through her body, making it harder for them to move quickly.

They came upon an old, abandoned house at the edge of the road. It loomed in the darkness, its windows shattered and the door hanging off its hinges. Desperate for shelter, they decided to take refuge inside.

The house was decrepit and filled with creepy relics—old photographs, broken furniture, and a thick layer of dust covering everything. Strange noises echoed through the halls, the creaking of the floorboards and the distant sound of whispering.

Sarah helped Jenna to a tattered couch, trying to treat her wounds with the limited supplies they had. "We'll rest here for a bit," Sarah said, her voice shaky. "Just try to stay awake."

As Sarah searched the house for anything useful, she stumbled upon a dusty old photograph hidden in a drawer. It was a picture of the clown, but in the photo, it looked happy and human. The back of the photo was inscribed with a name and date: "Arthur Greene, 1923."

Sarah's heart pounded as she pieced together the truth. The clown was once a renowned performer named Arthur Greene, who had been murdered by jealous carnival workers. His spirit had cursed the carnival, seeking revenge on anyone who entered.

"Jenna, you need to see this," Sarah said, rushing back to the living room.

But Jenna was writhing in pain, her body reacting violently to the clown's curse. Her skin began to pale, and her eyes took on a crazed gleam. "Sarah... I don't feel right," she gasped.

Jenna's transformation was horrifying. Her features twisted and contorted, her teeth elongating into sharp points. Her eyes glowed with a malevolent light, and she let out a maniacal laugh that chilled Sarah to the bone.

"Jenna, no!" Sarah cried, backing away in terror.

From the shadows, the real clown emerged, its grin wider and more sinister than ever. "Did you really think you could escape?" it taunted. "She belongs to me now."

A bloody showdown ensued. Sarah fought desperately, using anything she could find as a weapon. Jenna, now a grotesque clown-like creature, attacked with a ferocity that seemed unstoppable. The real clown watched with glee, savoring the chaos.

In a final, desperate act, Sarah managed to grab a broken piece of wood and drove it into the real clown's chest. The clown let out a piercing scream, its body convulsing as it dissolved into ash.

But the victory was hollow. Jenna, mortally wounded in the struggle, collapsed to the floor. "Sarah..." she whispered, her eyes flickering with a moment of clarity before they closed forever.

Sarah's tears flowed freely as she cradled her friend's lifeless body. The house around her began to collapse, the curse's grip loosening with the clown's destruction.

Stumbling out of the ruins, Sarah felt a strange sensation wash over her. The clown's laughter echoed in her mind, and she realized with dawning horror that she had been marked by the curse. The nightmare was far from over.

As she walked into the night, the echoes of the clown's sinister laughter followed her, promising that the terror would continue.

Sanctuary of Shadows

Chapter 1

The Unholy Presence

The old church loomed over the small, isolated town, its once grand facade now crumbling and overgrown with ivy. It had been abandoned for decades, left to decay and become a local legend. Emily, a dedicated historian, had convinced her friend David, a photographer, and Claire, their skeptical companion, to join her in documenting its history and rumored hauntings.

As they approached the church, the sun dipped below the horizon, casting long shadows that seemed to stretch and twist unnaturally. Emily clutched her notebook tightly, her excitement barely masking a deep sense of unease. David adjusted his camera, capturing the eerie beauty of the building, while Claire shivered and pulled her coat tighter around her.

"Are you sure about this, Emily?" Claire asked, her voice tinged with apprehension.

"It'll be fine," Emily assured her. "We're just here to document the place. Nothing's going to happen."

They pushed open the heavy wooden doors, which groaned in protest, and stepped inside. The air was thick with dust and the scent of decay, the interior shrouded in darkness.

The church's interior was a haunting sight. Pews were overturned, and the altar was covered in cobwebs. Strange symbols were etched into the walls, their meanings lost to time. David's camera flashed, illuminating the shadows and capturing the eerie scene.

"Look at these symbols," Emily said, running her fingers over the carvings. "They must be centuries old."

David snapped photos while Emily poured over old, dusty texts she found scattered near the altar. "This place has a dark history," she murmured, reading aloud about the mysterious disappearances and tragic events that had plagued the church.

Meanwhile, Claire wandered deeper into the church, her footsteps echoing in the vast, empty space. She stumbled upon a hidden door behind the altar, its wooden surface worn and splintered.

"Guys, I found something," she called out.

The hidden door creaked open, revealing a narrow staircase leading down into the basement. The air grew colder as they descended, the oppressive darkness closing in around them. The basement was filled with old, bloodstained tools and strange markings on the floor.

David's camera captured the unsettling scene, the flash revealing more than their eyes could see. Whispers and faint footsteps echoed through the basement, but no one else was there.

"This place gives me the creeps," Claire whispered, her breath visible in the frigid air.

Emily nodded, feeling the oppressive presence growing stronger. "We need to document this quickly and get out."

Suddenly, a shadow moved at the edge of their vision. Before they could react, a human-like creature with demonic features emerged from the darkness. Its skin was pale and mottled, eyes glowing with malevolent fire, and its fingers ended in sharp, claw-like nails.

The creature lunged at David, its claws slashing through his shirt and into his flesh. He screamed in pain, falling to the ground as blood poured from his wounds. Emily and Claire watched in horror as the creature retreated into the shadows, its eyes never leaving them.

"We have to get out of here!" Claire screamed, helping David to his feet. He was bleeding heavily, his face pale and contorted with pain.

They rushed back up the stairs, but when they reached the main hall, the exits were mysteriously blocked. The heavy wooden doors refused to budge, and the windows were covered with thick, impenetrable boards.

"We're trapped," Emily whispered, her voice trembling. "That thing is still here."

The creature's presence was palpable, its oppressive aura filling the church. They could hear its guttural growls and the sound of its claws scraping against the stone floor.

Desperate, they searched for another way out, but the church seemed to twist and change, leading them in circles. The creature stalked them, its terrifying visage appearing and disappearing in the shadows.

The chapter ended with the creature cornering them in the basement, its eyes glowing with a sadistic glee. Their hearts pounded with terror as they realized the true horror of their situation: they were trapped in the church with a demonic entity that had no intention of letting them leave alive.

Chapter 2

The Demon's Wrath

The creature's growls echoed through the dark, abandoned church, sending shivers down Emily, David, and Claire's spines. They could feel its malevolent presence stalking them, the oppressive atmosphere pressing down on them like a vise.

"We need to split up," David gasped, clutching his bleeding side. "We can cover more ground that way."

Reluctantly, they agreed, each heading in a different direction in a desperate attempt to find another way out. The church seemed to come alive with whispers and shadowy figures that flitted around them, their fear intensifying with every passing second.

Emily stumbled into an old chapel within the church, its air thick with decay and dread. Grotesque statues loomed over her, their faces twisted into expressions of agony and horror. The walls were adorned with unsettling relics, and strange symbols glowed faintly in the dim light.

The oppressive atmosphere grew heavier, and Emily's heart pounded in her chest. Suddenly, the creature attacked, its claws slashing through the air. She grabbed a heavy candlestick and swung it with all her might, striking the creature and causing it to retreat momentarily.

Her victory was short-lived, but it bought her precious moments to escape.

Meanwhile, David, weakened by his injuries, found himself lost in a dark, narrow passage. His vision blurred as he stumbled forward, each step more painful than the last. Horrific visions assailed him: scenes of the church's dark past and the creature feasting on its hapless victims.

He could hear the creature closing in, its footsteps echoing ominously. With a surge of adrenaline, David turned to face his pursuer, but the creature was too fast. It lunged at him, knocking him to the ground. The confrontation was brutal, with David fighting desperately, but his strength was failing.

Claire wandered through the labyrinthine halls, her mind racing with fear. She stumbled into a room filled with old, bloodstained robes and ritualistic tools. The air was thick with the stench of death, and the walls seemed to pulse as if alive.

Panic set in as the room began to close in on her, the shadows deepening. The creature's whispers filled her ears, tormenting her with shadowy apparitions. Her sanity frayed, and she could feel herself teetering on the edge of madness.

"Emily! David!" she screamed, her voice echoing off the walls, but only the creature's mocking laughter answered her.

Emily, armed with a makeshift weapon, finally found David. He lay on the floor, mortally wounded and barely conscious. Tears streamed down her face as she tried to help him up, her heart breaking at the sight of his pain.

"We have to find Claire," David whispered, his voice weak.

They stumbled through the dark halls, their progress slow and agonizing. They found Claire in the ritual room, her eyes wide with terror and her mind on the brink of collapse. Together, they faced the creature once more, realizing they had no choice but to confront it.

The creature cornered them, its eyes glowing with sadistic glee. The final showdown was brutal and bloody. Emily swung her weapon with all her might, David fought through his pain, and Claire, driven by sheer terror, joined the fray.

The creature's roars filled the church, shaking the very walls. Blood splattered across the floor as the battle raged on. Emily felt her strength waning, but she refused to give up. In a climactic moment, they managed to wound the creature severely, but the cost was high.

The chapter ended with the group battered and bleeding, their fate uncertain as the creature lay defeated but not dead. The oppressive atmosphere lingered, and the true horror of their situation settled over them like a dark cloud.

Chapter 3

The Abyssal Nightmare

The creature, though severely wounded, began to regenerate before their eyes. Its flesh knitted together with sickening speed, and its glowing eyes locked onto the group once more. Emily, David, and Claire exchanged horrified glances, realizing the creature was far more resilient than they had imagined.

The church itself seemed to respond to the creature's resurgence. The walls twisted and distorted, the architecture warping into a nightmarish labyrinth. Hallways stretched into infinity, doors appeared and disappeared, and the very air seemed to vibrate with malevolent energy.

"We need to keep moving," Emily urged, her voice trembling. "It's not going to stop."

They stumbled into a long hall filled with shifting shadows and eerie, distorted echoes of their own voices. The shadows danced and writhed, taking on monstrous forms that lunged at them from the darkness. The hall seemed alive, feeding off their fear.

As the shadows attacked, the group was driven apart. Emily swung her makeshift weapon at the apparitions, but her strikes passed through them like smoke. David and Claire fought desperately, but the shadows overwhelmed them, pulling them in different directions.

"Stay together!" Emily shouted, but her voice was swallowed by the darkness.

David, gravely injured and realizing he couldn't go on much longer, made a fateful decision. He would make a last stand to give Emily and Claire a chance to escape. "Go! I'll hold it off!" he yelled, his voice filled with determination.

"David, no!" Emily cried, but it was too late. David charged at the creature, using his remaining strength to fight it. The battle was brutal and hopelessly one-sided. The creature tore into David with savage fury, his screams echoing through the church.

His sacrifice bought Emily and Claire precious time, but the creature's bloodlust was undeterred. It resumed its hunt, more enraged than ever.

Claire began to lose her grip on reality. The church's malevolent influence seeped into her mind, distorting her perceptions. She saw horrific visions: walls dripping with blood, dismembered bodies, and grotesque figures lurking in the corners of her vision.

She heard voices whispering her name, mocking her, and predicting her doom. The line between reality and nightmare blurred, and she saw visions of her own death—her body torn apart by the creature, her blood painting the walls.

"Claire, focus!" Emily pleaded, trying to keep her grounded. But the church's influence was overpowering, and Claire's sanity frayed with each passing moment.

They finally reached the heart of the church, a cavernous room filled with bloodstained altars and demonic statues. The air was thick with the scent of decay and blood. The creature reappeared, more monstrous and enraged than ever, its eyes burning with malevolent fire.

Emily and Claire stood their ground, using everything at their disposal to fight the creature. The battle was savage and bloody. Emily swung her weapon with desperate strength, while Claire fought with a ferocity born of sheer terror.

The creature's claws raked across Emily's chest, and she fell to the ground, blood pouring from the wound. "Emily, no!" Claire screamed, her voice filled with despair.

In a climactic moment, Emily managed to land a devastating blow, wounding the creature severely. But the effort cost her dearly. She collapsed, mortally wounded, her breaths shallow and labored.

"Claire... run," Emily whispered, her voice fading.

The chapter ended with Claire standing alone, tears streaming down her face, as the creature loomed over her. The horror of their situation was complete: Emily lay dying, and Claire was left to face the demonic entity alone, with no hope of escape.

Chapter 4

The Descent into Madness

Claire was now alone, her breath coming in ragged gasps as she faced the full wrath of the creature. It no longer held back, its true malice unleashed upon her. The creature's form shifted and twisted, morphing into terrifying shapes that defied logic. One moment it was a monstrous humanoid, the next a writhing mass of darkness and teeth.

The church itself seemed to come alive, the walls warping and twisting as if they were flesh. Blood oozed from the cracks, pooling on the floor and staining her shoes. Demonic whispers filled the air, growing louder and more insistent with every step she took.

"You cannot escape," the creature's voice hissed, echoing from every direction. "You belong to me."

Claire stumbled into a vast hall filled with grotesque, rotting corpses posed in lifelike positions. Their faces were frozen in expressions of sheer terror, their eyes wide and unblinking. As she moved through the hall, she felt their eyes following her, watching her every move.

Her heart pounded in her chest, and she could feel the walls closing in around her. The creature's voice echoed through the hall, mocking her. "Look at them, Claire," it whispered. "They were all like you, and now they are mine."

Flashes of the creature's true, monstrous form appeared in the shadows, each more horrifying than the last. Its glowing eyes burned with malevolent intent, and its laughter sent chills down her spine.

She found herself standing before a massive, cracked mirror. The reflection that stared back at her was not her own, but a twisted, nightmarish version of herself. Each reflection showed her in various states of torment and death—dismembered, burning, drowning, screaming in agony.

The mirror seemed to pull her in, the visions becoming more real with each passing second. Claire's mind teetered on the brink of insanity as the horrific images overwhelmed her. "No... this isn't real," she whispered, but the mirror's grip was strong, and it threatened to trap her in the endless cycle of despair.

The mirror shattered, and Claire was thrown into the depths of the church, where she found herself in the creature's lair. It was a hellish room filled with the remnants of its past victims. Bones were scattered across the floor, and the walls were adorned with the faces of the dead, their mouths open in silent screams.

The creature emerged from the shadows, its form towering over her. It began to taunt her with visions of Emily and David, their faces twisted in pain and fear. They called out to her, their voices filled with desperation. "Help us, Claire... don't leave us here..."

Her resolve began to break. The creature's voice was relentless, its presence suffocating. She could feel the weight of the darkness pressing down on her, squeezing the life out of her.

In a last, desperate attempt to survive, Claire gathered what little strength she had left and confronted the creature. She had no weapon, no plan—only her willpower and the faint hope that she could somehow defeat it.

The creature revealed its true form, a nightmarish amalgamation of all the horrors she had faced. Its body was a mass of writhing flesh, teeth, and claws, its eyes burning with a hatred that seemed to pierce her very soul.

The final battle was brutal and chaotic. Claire fought with everything she had, her mind teetering on the edge of madness. The creature's claws tore at her, its teeth snapping inches from her face. The room seemed to twist and warp around them, the walls pulsating with dark energy.

Claire could feel herself slipping, her strength waning as the creature's relentless assault continued. The darkness closed in around her, the creature's laughter echoing in her ears. She knew she was losing, but she refused to give up.

With a final, desperate scream, Claire lunged at the creature, her fists connecting with its monstrous form. But it was too late. The creature's claws wrapped around her, dragging her into the depths of the church.

The chapter ended with Claire's screams fading into the darkness, the creature's laughter the only sound remaining as it consumed her completely. The church fell silent once more, the shadows reclaiming their territory, and the nightmare that had begun so long ago continued unabated.

Chapter 5

The Final Damnation

Claire awoke in complete darkness, her body aching and her mind disoriented. She was alone, the oppressive silence broken only by the distant, distorted voices that seemed to echo from all directions. The air was thick and foul, reeking of decay and something far worse.

As she reached out, her hands touched walls that felt like they were breathing, expanding and contracting with a sickening rhythm. Panic surged through her as she realized she was deep within the bowels of the church, trapped in a place that defied reality.

"Where am I?" she whispered, her voice trembling. But there was no answer, only the ever-present darkness and the feeling of being watched.

The darkness around her began to shift, and Claire was suddenly surrounded by visions of her friends—Emily and David. But something was horribly wrong. Their forms were twisted, their faces contorted into grotesque masks of pain and anger.

"Why did you leave us?" Emily's distorted voice accused, her eyes glowing with malice. "You could have saved us!"

David's broken form crawled toward her, blood pouring from his wounds. "This is your fault, Claire," he rasped. "You led us here."

The hallucinations grew more vivid, the voices louder, as they replayed the moments of their deaths, blaming her for everything. The walls seemed to close in, pressing down on her, suffocating her. Claire screamed, clutching her head as the madness threatened to consume her.

In her panic, Claire stumbled forward and found herself in a new chamber. The floor beneath her was wet and sticky, and as she looked down, she realized with horror that she was standing in waist-deep blood. The chamber was filled with it—warm, thick, and filled with dismembered body parts floating around her.

The walls pulsed and moaned, as if the church itself was alive and feeding on her fear. Claire waded through the blood, desperately trying to find an exit, but the chamber seemed endless, a grotesque maze designed to trap her forever.

"Please, no..." she whimpered, but the blood only grew thicker, the smell of death overwhelming.

The creature reappeared, emerging from the blood and shadows. It was no longer just a monstrous figure; its body had fused with the very walls of the church, becoming a grotesque amalgamation of flesh, stone, and darkness. Its eyes burned with a malevolent light as it gazed down at her.

"You were never meant to escape," the creature hissed, its voice a twisted mockery of human speech. "This church is not just a building. It is a living entity, a vessel for me—a gateway to the abyss."

Claire's blood ran cold as the creature continued, its voice dripping with sadistic glee. "You were always destined to become a part of it. Your suffering will feed me, and your soul will be trapped here for eternity."

Desperation fueled Claire's final attempt to fight back. She grabbed a floating piece of debris, swinging it wildly at the creature. But her efforts were futile. The creature's monstrous form enveloped her, its tendrils wrapping around her body, pulling her into its mass.

The pain was unbearable as the creature slowly and methodically tore her apart. Claire's screams echoed through the blood-filled chamber, her voice joining the chorus of tormented souls that had come before her. The creature fed on her fear, her agony, and her very essence.

In her final moments, Claire understood the full horror of her fate. She was now a part of the church, her soul trapped within its walls, doomed to suffer for eternity. The darkness closed in, and her consciousness faded into the abyss.

The church stood silent and ominous, its exterior giving no hint of the horrors within. But deep inside, the voices of the damned echoed endlessly, and Claire's voice joined them—a new addition to the twisted symphony of torment.

As the night fell, the church awaited its next victims, the creature within ever hungry, ever watchful, ready to consume anyone foolish enough to enter its cursed walls.

The Infection

Chapter 1

The Unseen Threat

Redwood was a town that time seemed to have forgotten. Nestled deep in the foothills of a mountain range and surrounded by dense, ancient forests, it was the kind of place where everyone knew each other, where the biggest news of the day might be a new diner special or a high school football game. The town's remote location kept it insulated from the world, and that was just the way the residents liked it.

Ethan was one of Redwood's few firefighters, a job that came with more downtime than action. Fires were rare, and the most excitement he usually saw was a cat stuck in a tree or a controlled burn that got out of hand. He enjoyed the peacefulness of it, the predictability. That morning, he sipped his coffee at the fire station, chatting with his colleagues about the upcoming town festival, completely unaware that everything was about to change.

Claire, a dedicated school teacher, was busy preparing for another day of classes. She loved her students and took pride in the tight-knit, supportive community of Redwood. The town's small size meant she knew every child by name, knew their families, their stories. It made teaching feel less like a job and more like a calling. That morning, she noticed a few of her students were absent, but didn't think much of it—it was flu season, after all.

Henry, the town's mayor, was preparing for his usual rounds, greeting the townsfolk and handling the day-to-day issues of Redwood. His role was more ceremonial than anything, given the town's small size, but he took it seriously. He saw himself as the town's guardian, ensuring that life in Redwood continued smoothly and safely. That morning, as he made his way to the town hall, he couldn't shake the feeling that something was off. The air felt heavy, and there was an eerie stillness that clung to the town like a fog.

But Redwood was a place of routine, and so the day began like any other, with no hint of the horror that was about to unfold.

Ethan's quiet morning was interrupted by the sound of the station's alarm bell. A call had come in about a fire on the outskirts of town. It wasn't a large fire, the dispatcher said, but it was in an odd location—right at the edge of the woods, where nothing should have been burning.

Ethan and his crew jumped into action, though the lack of urgency in the dispatcher's voice made them think it was probably just a small brush fire. When they arrived at the scene, however, they found something far stranger. The fire had already burned itself out, leaving behind a blackened patch of earth and an abandoned vehicle, its windows shattered and doors ajar.

There were scorch marks on the ground, but they weren't the result of a typical fire. They looked… deliberate, like something had been burned away with precision. And the vehicle… it was covered in strange, oily residue that Ethan couldn't identify. He felt a chill run down his spine as he inspected the scene, a sense of foreboding gnawing at him.

Meanwhile, across town, Claire was growing increasingly concerned. Several of her students hadn't shown up for class, and when she called their parents, she got no answer. By midday, the school had received word that more parents were missing, with no explanation as to where they might have gone. The children who were present seemed anxious, whispering to each other about strange things they had heard their parents talking about the night before—things about noises in the woods and lights in the sky.

At the same time, Henry was dealing with a flood of complaints from residents. Livestock had gone missing from several farms on the edge of town, and people were reporting strange sounds coming from the forest at night—low growls, rustling leaves, and the occasional distant scream. Henry tried to reassure everyone that it was probably just wild animals, maybe a bear or a mountain lion, but deep down, he felt a growing unease.

By afternoon, the sense of dread that had been simmering beneath the surface began to bubble over. The town of Redwood was no longer the quiet, peaceful place it had always been. Something was happening—something dark and unnatural.

It was late in the afternoon when the first real sign of the horror to come stumbled into town. Jacob, a local farmer known for his quiet demeanor and strong work ethic, staggered into the main square, his clothes torn and bloodied. His face was pale, his eyes wide with terror, and his breath came in ragged gasps. He was muttering incoherently, his words a jumbled mess that no one could make sense of.

People gathered around him, trying to help, but Jacob recoiled from their touch, as if in pain. "It's not… it's not right," he kept saying, over and over. "It's… alive, but it's not… it shouldn't be…"

Claire, who had been walking home from school, saw the commotion and rushed over. When she saw Jacob's condition, she immediately recognized the signs of shock and trauma. She tried to calm him down, but he suddenly convulsed, his body jerking violently. His eyes rolled back into his head, and he collapsed to the ground, his limbs twitching.

Someone shouted for help, and Henry, who had been nearby, ran over. Ethan, who had been returning to the station, arrived just in time to see Jacob's body go still. The townspeople stood around in stunned silence, unsure of what to do.

But before anyone could react, Jacob's body began to move again. This time, it was different. His movements were jerky, unnatural, as if his limbs were being pulled by invisible strings. Slowly, he rose to his feet, his head lolling to one side, his eyes glazed and unfocused.

"Jacob?" Henry called out, stepping forward cautiously. "Jacob, are you—?"

Jacob lunged at Henry with a speed and ferocity that took everyone by surprise. He tackled Henry to the ground, his mouth snapping open and closed like an animal. Ethan and several others rushed forward, pulling Jacob off of Henry, but it took all of their strength to hold him down. Jacob thrashed and snarled, his eyes wild and empty, his hands clawing at the ground.

Henry scrambled to his feet, his heart racing, as the townspeople struggled to contain Jacob. But as they did, Jacob let out a guttural growl, one that sent chills down everyone's spine. His body convulsed one last time, then went still.

For a moment, no one moved. The silence was thick, heavy with fear and confusion. And then, just as suddenly as it had started, it was over. Jacob was dead.

Or so they thought.

That night, the infection spread through Redwood like wildfire. Whatever had taken hold of Jacob was far more contagious—and far more deadly—than anyone could have imagined. People began to fall ill, their symptoms starting with high fever and uncontrollable shivers. But the illness didn't stop there. Soon, those infected began to exhibit violent, erratic behavior, attacking anyone who came near them.

Ethan, Claire, and Henry quickly realized that this was no ordinary illness. The town's small hospital was overrun with patients, many of whom succumbed to the infection and turned into ravenous zombies, attacking staff and other patients. The scenes of chaos and bloodshed were beyond anything they had ever seen.

Ethan and his fellow firefighters tried to help where they could, but it was clear that they were outmatched. The infected were relentless, their hunger insatiable. They tore through the town, leaving a trail of destruction in their wake. Homes were broken into, shops ransacked, and the streets ran red with blood.

Claire did her best to help the injured, but she was soon overwhelmed by the sheer number of people in need. She and a few other survivors barricaded themselves in the school, using desks and chairs to block the doors. They could hear the infected outside, their growls and snarls echoing through the empty hallways.

Henry coordinated efforts from the town hall, trying to organize a defense against the growing horde. But it was a losing battle. The infection was spreading too quickly, and the infected were too strong. They broke through barricades with ease, their bodies seemingly impervious to pain.

As night fell, Redwood was plunged into chaos. The infection had reached a critical point, and the town was overrun with bloodthirsty zombies. The streets were filled with screams, the sounds of breaking glass, and the sickening crunch of bones as the undead feasted on their victims.

Ethan, Claire, and Henry, along with a small group of other survivors, made their way to the town hall, their last hope for safety. They fortified the building as best they could, using whatever materials they could find to block the doors and windows. But the undead were relentless, pounding on the barricades with horrifying ferocity.

Inside, the survivors were terrified, their faces pale and their eyes wide with fear. They knew that if the zombies broke through, there would be no escape. They could hear the infected outside, their guttural growls and the sound of their claws scraping against the walls.

"We have to hold them off," Ethan said, his voice firm despite the fear gnawing at him. "We can't let them get in."

The group gathered whatever weapons they could find—guns, knives, even broken furniture. They prepared for the inevitable onslaught, knowing that their survival depended on their ability to fight back.

As the night wore on, the barricades began to give way. The infected broke through the doors, their eyes glowing with a malevolent hunger. The survivors fought with everything they had, but the undead were too many, their strength too great.

The chapter ended with the survivors facing a desperate fight for their lives as the town of Redwood was consumed by the outbreak. The once-peaceful town was now a battleground, and the night had become a blood-soaked nightmare.

Chapter 2

The Night of Terror

The barricades at the town hall groaned and buckled under the relentless assault of the undead. The pounding grew louder, the wood splintering, and the nails straining against the force. Ethan, Claire, Henry, and the other survivors braced themselves, weapons in hand, hearts pounding with fear.

With a deafening crash, the barricades gave way, and the undead flooded in. Their eyes glowed with a malevolent hunger, their mouths open in twisted snarls. The air was filled with the stench of decay and the guttural growls of the infected. The sight was nightmarish—bloody, rotting bodies moving with unnatural speed and ferocity.

"Hold them off!" Ethan shouted, firing his shotgun into the horde. The blast took down several zombies, but more kept coming, clawing over the bodies of their fallen.

Claire swung a crowbar, connecting with the head of an approaching zombie. The force of the blow sent it crashing to the ground, but another was right behind it, lunging at her with outstretched hands.

Henry fought with a grim determination, using a baseball bat to fend off the attackers. But it was clear they were being overwhelmed. The undead were relentless, their numbers seeming to grow with each passing second.

"Fall back!" Henry yelled. "Get to the upper floors!"

The survivors retreated up the stairs, the undead hot on their heels. The growls and snarls echoed through the building, the sound of their pursuit a constant reminder of the horror that awaited if they were caught.

The group split up, each taking different routes in a desperate attempt to find a way out. Claire led a small group to the roof, hoping to signal for help. As they emerged into the cool night air, they were met with a horrifying sight—the streets below were swarming with zombies. Hundreds of them, moving in a twisted dance of death, their moans filling the air.

"There's no way out," one of the survivors whispered, his voice trembling with fear.

Claire's heart sank. The sheer number of undead was overwhelming. She scanned the horizon, looking for any sign of hope, but there was none. They were trapped, surrounded by a sea of death.

Meanwhile, Ethan and Henry were attempting to secure a path through the lower levels. The hallways were dark, the only light coming from the flickering emergency bulbs. The shadows seemed to move, and every corner held the potential for an ambush.

"Stay close," Ethan whispered, his shotgun at the ready.

As they moved, the sounds of the undead grew louder. The infected were everywhere, their blood-soaked hands reaching from the darkness, their eyes glinting with a feral intelligence. It was as if the building itself had come alive with the intent to devour them.

In the chaos, one of the survivors, overwhelmed by fear, turned on the group. His eyes were wild, his face pale with terror. "We're all going to die!" he screamed. "I won't be their food!"

Before anyone could react, he shoved one of the others into the path of an approaching zombie. The infected tore into the unfortunate victim, their screams filling the air. The betrayal sent the group into disarray, and more zombies took advantage of the confusion, attacking from all sides.

"Stop him!" Henry shouted, grappling with the traitor. But the struggle only added to the chaos, and more lives were lost in the ensuing mayhem.
Ethan fired his shotgun, the blast taking down several zombies, but it was clear they were losing the fight. The group was thinning, their numbers dwindling as the undead picked them off one by one.

As the night wore on, the survivors' mental states began to deteriorate. The constant threat of death, the relentless pursuit of the undead, and the loss of their friends took a heavy toll. Hallucinations and paranoia set in, making it difficult to distinguish reality from nightmare.

Claire found herself seeing visions of her loved ones, their faces twisted into the grotesque forms of zombies. She saw her parents, her siblings, her friends—all turned into monsters, reaching out to her with bloody hands. The visions were so vivid, so real, that she couldn't tell if they were hallucinations or if the infection had somehow gotten to them too.

Ethan, too, was struggling. He saw shadows moving where there were none, heard whispers in the silence. The line between friend and foe blurred, and he found himself second-guessing every decision, every movement. The pressure was unbearable, the fear all-consuming.

Realizing that staying inside the town hall meant certain death, the group made a last-ditch effort to escape. They fought their way through the building, each encounter with the undead more brutal and bloody than the last. The hallways were slick with blood, the air filled with the stench of death and the sounds of battle.

In the chaos, Ethan and Claire were separated from the others. They moved through the darkened corridors, the moans of the undead echoing all around them. Every step was a battle, every moment a fight for survival.

They finally made it to a nearby house, barricading themselves inside. The silence was deafening, the sudden stillness almost surreal. They had found temporary refuge, but their relief was short-lived. They knew the undead were still out there, still hunting them. And they knew that the true horror had only just begun.

The chapter ended with Ethan and Claire huddled together in the darkness, the sounds of the undead outside growing louder, closer. They were trapped, surrounded by a nightmare with no end in sight.

Chapter 3

The Depths of Despair

Ethan and Claire sat in the dimly lit living room of the house, their breaths coming in shallow gasps. The night had been a relentless nightmare, and the silence that now surrounded them was almost as unsettling as the chaos they had fled. The house seemed abandoned, but there was a palpable sense of unease that clung to the air.

They began to explore, their flashlights casting long, flickering shadows on the walls. The signs of a violent struggle were everywhere—bloodstains smeared across the floors, broken furniture scattered throughout the rooms, and personal belongings left behind in a state of disarray.

Claire picked up a family photo from the floor, the glass frame cracked. The smiling faces of a man, woman, and two children stared back at her, now a haunting reminder of the lives that had been shattered by the outbreak. She shivered and placed the photo back down, trying to push the images of what might have happened to them out of her mind.

Ethan motioned for Claire to follow him. They moved cautiously through the house, their footsteps muffled by the thick carpet. Every creak of the floorboards and every rustle of the wind outside made them jump. The unsettling noises seemed to be coming from the basement, a low, persistent scratching that set their nerves on edge.

"Do you hear that?" Claire whispered, her voice trembling.

Ethan nodded, his grip tightening on the flashlight. "We need to check it out. There might be supplies down there."

Despite their fear, they knew they had no choice. They descended the narrow stairs to the basement, each step echoing in the confined space.

The basement was a place of nightmares. It was dark and damp, the air thick with a sickening stench that made them gag. Their flashlights revealed more signs of the previous occupants' gruesome fate—blood splatters on the walls, deep gouges in the floor, and discarded clothing soaked in red.

As they ventured deeper, they stumbled upon a grotesque sight. In a corner of the basement, half-hidden by shadows, was a mutilated body. But this was no ordinary zombie. It was a grotesque abomination, its flesh warped and twisted, eyes glowing with an unnatural light. The infection had evolved, turning it into something far more monstrous.

The creature lunged at them with terrifying speed. Ethan fired his shotgun, the blast echoing through the basement. The creature shrieked, but it kept coming, its claws slashing through the air. Claire swung her crowbar, the metal connecting with a sickening crunch, but the monster seemed unfazed.

The battle was brutal and bloody. The creature's strength was overwhelming, its attacks relentless. Ethan and Claire fought with everything they had, their weapons tearing into the creature's flesh. Finally, with a desperate swing of the crowbar, Claire managed to crush the creature's skull, its body collapsing to the ground in a twitching heap.

They stood over the corpse, their breaths ragged, their bodies shaking with adrenaline and fear. The basement was silent once more, but the memory of the battle would haunt them.

As they caught their breath, Ethan's flashlight beam fell on a dusty old radio sitting on a shelf. He picked it up, hoping against hope that it still worked. With a few adjustments and a lot of static, they managed to pick up a faint distress signal.

"…this is Alpha Base… attempting to quarantine… survivors… evacuation…"

The signal was weak and filled with static, but it was a lifeline. A nearby military outpost was trying to quarantine the area and evacuate any survivors. It was their best chance for survival.

"We have to get to that outpost," Ethan said, determination in his eyes. "It's our only hope."

Claire nodded, though the thought of leaving the relative safety of the house filled her with dread. The journey would be perilous, but staying meant certain death.

They prepared to leave, gathering what supplies they could find. As they stepped out into the night, the full scope of the horror around them became clear. The streets were filled with scenes of unimaginable terror—buildings burning, piles of corpses, and the haunting moans of the undead.

The zombies were everywhere, each one more terrifying and aggressive than the last. Their eyes glowed with a malevolent light, their movements unnaturally fast and coordinated. Ethan and Claire moved cautiously, their weapons at the ready, but it felt like the undead were watching, waiting for the perfect moment to strike.

They were forced to take shelter in an old church, its stained glass windows casting eerie, distorted light on the pews below. Inside, they found another group of survivors huddled together. Relief washed over them, but it was short-lived.

The survivors seemed friendly at first, but there was something off about them. Their eyes were wild, their bodies gaunt and hungry. As the night wore on, Ethan and Claire realized the horrifying truth—the group was not what they seemed.

The survivors revealed their true nature in a terrifying betrayal. They were cannibals, preying on the living to survive. The realization hit Ethan and Claire like a punch to the gut, their stomachs turning with disgust and fear.

"You won't make it out there," the leader of the group sneered, a twisted smile on his face. "Stay with us, and you might live a little longer."

But Ethan and Claire knew they couldn't stay. They had to escape, no matter the cost. The church, once a place of sanctuary, had become a death trap. They fought their way out, the battle bloody and desperate. The cannibals were ruthless, but the undead were even more relentless, breaking into the church and attacking everyone inside.

In the chaos, Ethan and Claire managed to slip away, but not without injury. Bloodied and exhausted, they made their way through the town, each step a fight for survival. They knew their situation was growing increasingly dire, but they also knew they couldn't give up.

The chapter ended with Ethan and Claire finding temporary refuge in an abandoned house. They tended to their wounds, their bodies and minds exhausted from the night's horrors. But as they looked out the window, they saw the blood-red glow of the sunrise, a reminder that the true terror had only just begun.

Chapter 4

The Descent into Hell

Ethan and Claire, though exhausted and wounded, knew they couldn't stay in the abandoned house for long. As the first light of dawn crept through the broken windows, they steeled themselves for the journey ahead. Their destination: the military outpost they had heard about on the radio. It was their only hope.

The forest surrounding Redwood, once a place of beauty and tranquility, had become a twisted labyrinth of terror. The dense canopy above cast long, eerie shadows that danced and whispered in the morning light. Every rustle of leaves, every snapping twig set their nerves on edge.

As they moved through the underbrush, they encountered the remains of other survivors who hadn't been as lucky. Bodies lay grotesquely mutilated, their faces frozen in expressions of unimaginable horror. The sight was a grim reminder of the dangers that lay ahead.

"Keep moving," Ethan whispered, his voice strained. "We can't afford to stop."

Claire nodded, though her eyes were wide with fear. The air was thick with tension, every step forward a battle against the creeping dread that threatened to overwhelm them.

As they ventured deeper into the forest, the shadows seemed to grow darker, more oppressive. Suddenly, from the darkness, an abomination emerged—a monstrous, evolved zombie with horrific mutations. Its skin was covered in grotesque growths, its limbs elongated and twisted, eyes glowing with a malevolent intelligence.

The creature moved with terrifying speed, blending with the shadows, its snarls echoing through the trees. Ethan and Claire barely had time to react before it was upon them, claws slashing through the air.

Ethan fired his shotgun, the blast tearing into the creature's flesh, but it barely slowed down. Claire swung her crowbar, the metal connecting with a sickening crunch, but the abomination seemed almost impervious to pain.

The fight was brutal and bloody. The creature's strength and ferocity were overwhelming, every attack a desperate struggle for survival. Blood sprayed across the forest floor as they fought, each blow pushing them closer to exhaustion.

Finally, with a last, desperate effort, they managed to bring the creature down, its body collapsing in a heap of twitching limbs. Ethan and Claire stood over it, their breaths coming in ragged gasps, their bodies shaking with adrenaline and fear.

"This infection… it's evolving," Claire whispered, her voice trembling. "What are we dealing with?"

Ethan shook his head, unable to find the words. They were facing something far worse than they had ever imagined.

They pressed on, their bodies battered and bleeding, until they stumbled upon an old, abandoned cabin in the middle of the forest. The cabin offered a fragile sanctuary, a place to tend to their wounds and regroup.

Inside, the air was thick with the smell of decay and old wood. The walls were covered in strange symbols, relics of dark rituals left behind by the previous inhabitants. It was clear that those who had lived here had tried to control or appease the infection, but their efforts had ended in horror.

As night fell, Ethan and Claire were haunted by nightmarish visions. The whispers in the dark grew louder, filling their minds with images of twisted, undead faces and blood-soaked landscapes. Reality and hallucination blurred, leaving them questioning their own sanity.

"Do you hear that?" Claire whispered, her eyes darting around the room.

Ethan nodded, his grip tightening on his shotgun. The whispers seemed to be coming from all around them, an endless chorus of malevolent voices.

The whispers grew louder, leading a swarm of zombies to the cabin. The undead launched a relentless assault, breaking through doors and windows with terrifying ease. Their eyes glowed with an insatiable hunger, their growls filling the air.

Ethan and Claire fought desperately to defend their fragile sanctuary. The battle was chaotic and gruesome, blood and flesh flying as they swung their weapons with all their remaining strength. The zombies were more vicious and coordinated than ever, their attacks relentless.

"Fall back!" Ethan shouted, firing into the horde. "We can't hold them off!"

They retreated deeper into the cabin, but it was no use. The undead broke through every barrier, their blood-soaked hands reaching for them. The cabin was overrun, consumed by the swarm of zombies.

In a final, desperate effort, Ethan and Claire managed to escape through a broken window, their bodies bruised and bleeding. They ran through the forest, the sounds of the undead fading behind them.

On the run again, they stumbled upon a hidden underground bunker, a remnant of an old military installation. The heavy metal door creaked open, revealing a dark, musty interior. Inside, the air was thick with the scent of chemicals and decay.

As they explored the bunker, they discovered horrifying experiments and evidence that the infection may have been man-made. Documents and research notes suggested it was a bioweapon, an experiment gone horribly wrong.

The bunker was filled with failed experiments—mutated zombies and abominations, all locked behind thick glass and steel. Their eyes followed Ethan and Claire as they moved through the corridors, their snarls and growls echoing in the confined space. "This… this is where it started," Claire whispered, horror dawning in her eyes.

Ethan nodded, his face pale. "And it's spreading."

The chapter ended with a chilling revelation: the infection was spreading beyond Redwood, and the world was on the brink of a global apocalypse. The true horror had only just begun.

Chapter 5

The End of Hope

Ethan and Claire stood in the heart of the bunker, surrounded by the remnants of twisted experiments and dark, secretive research. The walls were lined with cages and tanks, each one containing horrors beyond imagination. They knew that the infection had to be contained, but the scale of what they were facing was overwhelming.

"We have to destroy this place," Ethan said, his voice resolute. "If this gets out... the world won't stand a chance."

Claire nodded, her eyes filled with determination. "We need to find the main control room. If we can overload the system, we might be able to take the whole place down."

As they moved deeper into the bunker, they found more grotesque experiments—mutated zombies, their bodies warped and fused with machinery, and creatures that defied description. The air was thick with the scent of decay and chemicals, a nauseating reminder of the atrocities committed here.

Suddenly, the radio crackled to life. A distress call from the military outpost came through, urging any survivors to reach the evacuation point before the area was bombed to contain the outbreak.

"This is our chance," Claire said, her voice urgent. "We have to get out of here."

Ethan and Claire quickly gathered supplies and weapons, knowing that the journey to the evacuation point would be perilous. They mapped out a route, but the path was fraught with dangers, and the odds were stacked against them.

As they prepared to leave, the mutated zombies contained in the bunker broke free, their restraints no longer holding them back. The creatures were a nightmare made flesh—grotesque abominations with claws and fangs, moving with unnatural speed.

The fight was brutal and bloody. Ethan fired his shotgun, the blasts echoing through the narrow corridors, but the creatures were relentless. Claire swung her crowbar, the metal connecting with sickening thuds, but the zombies kept coming.

They fought with everything they had, their bodies battered and bleeding. The basement became a slaughterhouse, the walls painted with the blood of both the undead and the living. But they managed to push through, escaping the bunker just as the creatures overwhelmed it.

The journey to the evacuation point was a nightmarish gauntlet. The forest and town were filled with the undead, each encounter more terrifying than the last. The landscape was littered with the bodies of fallen survivors and burning wreckage, a grim testament to the devastation.

Every step was a fight for survival. The undead swarmed them, their eyes glowing with hunger, their mouths dripping with blood. Ethan and Claire's bodies and spirits were pushed to the brink, their strength waning with each passing moment.

"We're almost there," Ethan said, his voice hoarse. "Just a little further."

Claire nodded, though exhaustion was etched on her face. They moved forward, determined to reach the evacuation point, despite the overwhelming odds.

When they finally reached the evacuation point, their hearts sank. The area was overrun with zombies, and the military's efforts to contain the outbreak were failing. Soldiers fought desperately, their guns blazing, but the undead were too many, too relentless.

Ethan and Claire joined the fight, their weapons tearing into the horde. But it was clear that they were fighting a losing battle. The zombies swarmed the area, their numbers overwhelming.
In the chaos, Claire was mortally wounded, a zombie's claws raking across her abdomen. She fell to the ground, blood pouring from the wound.

"Ethan… go," she gasped, her voice weak. "You have to make it."

Tears streamed down Ethan's face as he held her. "I'm not leaving you," he said, his voice choked with emotion.

"You have to," Claire whispered. "Save yourself… for both of us."

With a heart-wrenching cry, Ethan kissed her forehead and stood up. He fought his way through the horde, his mind numb with grief and rage. Claire's screams echoed in his ears as he made his way to the evacuation helicopter.

As Ethan reached the helicopter, a soldier grabbed his arm. "Get in, we're leaving!"

Ethan climbed aboard, his heart heavy with loss. But as the helicopter lifted off, he noticed something strange—the soldiers weren't heading for safety. They were circling back towards the town.

"What are you doing?" Ethan shouted. "We need to get out of here!"

The soldier looked at him with cold eyes. "Orders are to gather as many infected as possible. We're not evacuating—we're testing."

Ethan's blood ran cold. "Testing? What do you mean?"

"The evacuation is a trap," the soldier said. "We're gathering the infected here for an experimental bombing. The goal is to find a cure, but it's a one-way trip."

Panic gripped Ethan as he realized the horrifying truth. The helicopter wasn't heading for safety—it was a death sentence. He looked out the window and saw the bombs falling, a series of bright flashes lighting up the ground below.

"No!" Ethan screamed, but it was too late. The bombs exploded, incinerating the area and everyone in it. The helicopter was caught in the blast, a fiery inferno consuming everything.

The chapter ended with the revelation that the infection had already spread globally. The efforts to contain it were futile, and the world was plunged into an apocalyptic nightmare. The last thing Ethan saw before the flames engulfed him was the blood-red sky, a harbinger of the end of humanity.

Silent Terror

Chapter 1

The Unseen Menace

Pine Haven was the kind of town where everyone knew everyone, a secluded haven surrounded by dense forests and towering mountains. Life moved at a leisurely pace, with days filled with the sounds of birds singing and leaves rustling in the wind. It was a place of peace and simplicity, far removed from the chaos of the outside world.

Alex was one of the town's park rangers, a job that suited him perfectly. He spent his days patrolling the forests, ensuring the trails were safe and the wildlife undisturbed. He loved the tranquility of the woods, the way the sunlight filtered through the trees, casting dappled shadows on the ground.

Julia was a teacher at the local school, dedicated to her students and the community. She had moved to Pine Haven to escape the hustle and bustle of the city, finding solace in the town's quiet charm. Her days were filled with lessons and laughter, the classroom a place of learning and growth.

Mike, the town's sheriff, took pride in keeping Pine Haven safe. His duties were usually mundane, dealing with minor disputes and ensuring the town's tranquility. But he enjoyed the simplicity of his work, the sense of security it brought to the community.

It was a typical day in Pine Haven, the residents going about their routines, unaware of the dark menace that was about to shatter their peace.

Alex was the first to notice something amiss. While patrolling the forest, he stumbled upon a series of strange animal carcasses. The bodies were mutilated, torn apart in ways that suggested something far more sinister than a predator. The wounds were deep, precise, as if inflicted by something with immense strength and sharp claws.

He reported his findings to Mike, who took the matter seriously. They had never seen anything like it before, and the thought of a dangerous creature lurking in the woods was unsettling. They decided to keep an eye on the situation, hoping it was an isolated incident.

Meanwhile, Julia noticed that several of her students had stopped coming to school. Concerned, she visited their homes, only to find them abandoned. The houses were eerily silent, as if the families had left in a hurry, leaving behind personal belongings and half-eaten meals. The air was thick with an unspoken dread, the sense that something terrible had happened.

Mike began receiving reports of strange noises at night—unnatural, guttural sounds that sent chills down the spines of those who heard them. Residents were disappearing without a trace, their homes left in disarray. The town was on edge, fear creeping into the hearts of the people.

The peace of Pine Haven was shattered one night when the creature struck. It moved through the town with terrifying speed and precision, drawn to any noise. The residents, awakened by the screams of their neighbors, looked out to see a monstrous figure silhouetted against the moonlit sky.

The creature was massive, its body twisted and grotesque. It had long, razor-sharp claws and a face scarred and deformed. Despite its blindness, it moved with unnerving accuracy, honing in on every sound. The attacks were brutal, the bodies of the victims mutilated beyond recognition.

Panic spread through the town like wildfire. People ran from their homes, desperate to escape the unseen menace. The creature followed, each noise leading it to another victim. The night was filled with screams and the sounds of tearing flesh, the once-peaceful town now a scene of unimaginable horror.

By dawn, several residents were dead, their bodies scattered across the streets. The survivors gathered at the town hall, their faces pale with fear. They knew they were dealing with something far beyond their understanding.

At the town hall, Alex, Julia, and Mike took charge. They knew they had to act quickly to protect the town. They discussed what little they knew about the creature—it was blind, drawn to noise, and immensely powerful.

"We have to hunt it," Alex said, his voice firm. "We can't wait for it to come back. We need to take the fight to it."

Mike nodded. "We'll use traps, weapons, anything we can find. But we have to stay silent. Any noise will bring it straight to us."

Julia, though terrified, agreed. "We need to protect the children, the families. We can't let it take any more lives."

They set to work, gathering supplies and preparing traps. They shared their plan with the rest of the town, urging everyone to remain as silent as possible. The sense of urgency was palpable, every creak of the floorboards and whisper in the hall a reminder of the danger that lurked outside.

As night fell, Alex, Julia, Mike, and a few other brave souls set out into the forest. They moved silently, using hand signals and whispers to communicate. The forest was dark and foreboding, every rustle of leaves and snap of a twig a potential death sentence.

They followed the trail of destruction left by the creature, the broken branches and bloodstains leading them deeper into the woods. The tension was palpable, every step filled with dread. They knew the creature was out there, waiting, listening.

Finally, they came upon a cave, its entrance hidden by thick underbrush. Inside, the air was thick with the stench of decay. Bones and remains littered the ground, the grisly trophies of the creature's previous attacks. The walls were stained with blood, the remnants of the monster's feeding frenzy.

"This is it," Mike whispered, his voice barely audible. "This is its lair."

The true horror of what they were up against became clear. The creature was not just a mindless beast—it was a predator, intelligent and deadly. They knew that one wrong move could mean their end.

The chapter ended with the group steeling themselves for the battle ahead, their resolve unshaken despite the overwhelming fear. They were determined to protect their town, no matter the cost. The fight for Pine Haven's survival had only just begun.

Chapter 2

The Hunt in the Shadows

The entrance to the cave loomed before them, a gaping maw in the earth that seemed to swallow all light. Alex, Julia, Mike, and the remaining members of their group steeled themselves before stepping into the darkness. The air inside was cold and damp, carrying the stench of decay and death.

Their flashlights cut through the inky blackness, revealing the narrow, twisting passages of the cave. Every step echoed ominously, the sound magnified by the enclosed space. The group moved cautiously, their nerves on edge, every sense heightened.

As they ventured deeper, they found more evidence of the creature's previous attacks. Bones, shredded clothing, and personal items from the missing townsfolk littered the ground, grim reminders of the monster's brutality. The walls were stained with old blood, the remnants of the creature's feeding frenzy.

Alex set up traps as they moved, using his knowledge of hunting to create makeshift snares and tripwires. Julia and Mike kept watch, their weapons at the ready, every sound making their hearts race.

"We need to be careful," Mike whispered, his voice barely audible. "One wrong move, and we're dead."

The silence was shattered by a sudden, deafening roar. The creature ambushed them with terrifying speed and ferocity, its massive form emerging from the shadows. It was even more monstrous up close—long, razor-sharp claws, a grotesque, twisted body covered in scars, and a face that seemed to be a patchwork of deformed flesh.

The confined space of the cave made the fight brutal and desperate. The creature's claws and teeth tore through flesh, its strength overwhelming. The group fought back with everything they had, their weapons slashing and striking the beast, but it seemed almost impervious to pain.

One of the group members, Tom, was caught off guard. The creature lunged at him, its claws ripping into his chest. His screams echoed through the cave, a horrifying reminder of their peril. Blood sprayed across the walls as Tom fell, his body convulsing in agony before going still.

"Tom!" Julia screamed, but there was nothing they could do. The creature turned its attention to the rest of them, its eyes glowing with a malevolent hunger.

Realizing they were outmatched, Alex shouted, "We have to retreat! Use the traps to slow it down!"

The group moved quickly, setting off the traps as they retreated. The creature roared in frustration as it hit the snares and tripwires, but it was relentless, pursuing them through the narrow passages.

The escape was a desperate scramble. The narrow passages made it difficult to move quickly, and the creature was always just behind them, its growls echoing in the confined space. They stumbled over rocks and debris, their breaths coming in ragged gasps.

They finally burst out of the cave, the fresh air hitting them like a wave of relief. But their relief was short-lived. They had lost more group members in the retreat, and those who remained were badly injured, their bodies bloodied and bruised.

"We can't fight it in there," Alex said, his voice grim. "It's too strong, too fast."

"We need a new plan," Mike agreed, his face pale with exhaustion. "And we need it fast."

Back in Pine Haven, the survivors regrouped at the town hall, tending to their wounds. The reality of their situation was sinking in. The creature was not confined to the cave. It could strike anywhere, at any time.

The town fell into an uneasy silence. People whispered, afraid to make any noise that might attract the monster. Doors were locked, windows were shuttered, and the streets were deserted. The once-vibrant community was now a ghost town, the fear palpable in the air.

Alex, Julia, and Mike knew they had to act. They couldn't live in constant fear, waiting for the creature to strike again. They had to find a way to kill it.

"We need to lure it into a trap," Alex said, his mind racing. "We need to use its weakness—its reliance on sound—against it."

They spent the next day preparing. They rigged a generator to create a loud noise, hoping to draw the creature to a specific location where they had set up an ambush. It was a risky plan, but it was their only hope.

Night fell, casting the town in shadows. The generator was set up in the town square, its loud hum breaking the silence. The group took their positions, weapons at the ready, every muscle tense with anticipation.

The noise echoed through the town, a beacon for the monster. It didn't take long for the creature to appear, its monstrous form silhouetted against the moonlight. It moved with terrifying grace, drawn to the sound like a moth to a flame.

"Get ready," Alex whispered, his grip tightening on his shotgun.

The creature approached, its claws clicking against the pavement. It stopped, its head tilting as it listened. The group held their breath, the tension unbearable.

Then, with a sudden, deafening roar, the creature lunged at the generator, its claws tearing into the metal. The trap was sprung. Explosions and gunfire filled the air as the group attacked, their weapons aimed at the monster.

The fight was chaotic and bloody. The creature thrashed and roared, its claws slashing through the air. Blood sprayed across the ground as they struck it, their attacks relentless. But the creature was incredibly resilient, its strength seeming to grow with each passing moment.

As the battle raged on, it became clear that the creature was not just a mindless beast. It was intelligent, adapting to their tactics, using the environment to its advantage. It turned its attention to the group, its eyes filled with a malevolent intelligence.

The chapter ended with the creature breaking through their defenses, its claws slashing through the air as the group fought desperately to survive. The night was filled with the sounds of battle, the once-peaceful town now a scene of unimaginable horror. The fight for Pine Haven's survival had reached its most critical point.

Chapter 3

The Monster's Wrath

The town square, once a place of community gatherings and peaceful afternoons, had transformed into a battleground. The trap they had painstakingly prepared had failed to kill the creature, and now it was all they could do to survive. The creature, massive and grotesque, moved with a horrifying intelligence. It used the darkness and debris to its advantage, its long claws scraping against the pavement, echoing like a death knell through the night.

"Stay together!" Alex shouted, but his voice was drowned out by the chaos.

The creature struck with terrifying speed, its claws slashing through the air, ripping through flesh and bone with sickening ease. Blood splattered across the cobblestones as one of the group members was torn apart, their scream cut short in a gurgling choke. The creature's eyes, though blind, seemed to track every movement with unerring accuracy, guided by the smallest sounds.

Julia, breathless and terrified, watched as the group was scattered, each survivor forced to flee in different directions. The night was filled with the sounds of their desperate retreat, the creature's guttural growls growing louder as it pursued them through the narrow streets of Pine Haven.

The town had become a deadly maze, each corner and alleyway a potential death trap. The survivors moved in terrified silence, their hearts pounding in their chests, their breaths shallow and controlled. The creature stalked them, its acute hearing making it nearly impossible to avoid detection.

Julia and Alex, their faces pale with fear, were separated from Mike in the chaos. They crouched behind a row of parked cars, every muscle tensed, listening as the creature's heavy footsteps echoed down the street.

Mike, realizing the creature was getting too close to Julia and Alex, decided to create a distraction. He grabbed a rock and threw it into the distance, the noise startling the creature. It turned sharply, its head tilting as it focused on the new sound.

"Come on, you bastard," Mike muttered under his breath, before taking off in the opposite direction, deliberately making noise to draw the creature away. He knew it was a gamble, but it was the only way to give the others a chance.

Julia and Alex took advantage of the distraction, slipping into a side alley and moving as quickly and quietly as they could. But the creature was relentless, and they knew it was only a matter of time before it found them again.

They found temporary refuge in the school, the building's darkened hallways offering some semblance of safety. The silence inside was oppressive, the walls seeming to close in around them. Julia and Alex moved cautiously, their flashlights revealing a trail of destruction that suggested the creature had already been there.

The classrooms were a nightmare. Desks were overturned, windows shattered, and the walls were stained with blood. Torn clothing and personal items lay scattered across the floor, evidence of a previous massacre. The sight was enough to make Julia gag, the horror of what had happened here almost too much to bear.

"We need to find a place to hide," Alex whispered, his voice trembling.

But before they could move, they heard it—the unmistakable sound of the creature's claws scraping against the floor. It had followed them into the school, drawn by the faintest noise they had made. The realization hit them like a physical blow: they were trapped in a building with a monster that could hear every breath, every heartbeat.

The next few moments were a terrifying game of cat and mouse. The creature moved through the hallways, its movements precise and deliberate. Julia and Alex did their best to stay silent, their hearts pounding in their chests as they hid in the shadows. But the creature was close—too close.

Meanwhile, Mike, in his effort to lead the creature away, stumbled upon something horrifying. As he fled through the streets, he noticed an entrance to what seemed like an old, forgotten underground passage. Driven by desperation, he ventured inside, hoping it would lead him somewhere safe.

But what he found was far from sanctuary. The passage led to a hidden chamber beneath the town—a lair filled with the remains of the creature's victims. Bones and body parts were strewn about, some piled in grotesque mounds, others arranged in disturbing patterns. The walls were covered in symbols scratched into the stone, symbols that seemed to pulse with a dark, malevolent energy.

The air was thick with the stench of death, and Mike felt a wave of nausea wash over him. He realized with growing horror that the creature was not just a mindless beast—it was something far worse. The lair was a grotesque shrine to death, a place where the creature brought its victims not just to feed, but to perform some kind of twisted ritual.

"This isn't just about survival," Mike whispered to himself, his voice shaking. "It's… it's something else. Something evil."

The realization chilled him to the bone. The creature was hunting them, yes, but it was also driven by a purpose that he couldn't comprehend—a purpose that seemed to be tied to the very town of Pine Haven itself.

Back in the school, Julia and Alex's situation had become dire. The creature was closing in, its claws clicking against the tiled floor, the sound like nails on a chalkboard. They were cornered, trapped in a small storage room with nowhere to run.

As the creature approached, it began to display a new and terrifying ability: it mimicked sounds and voices, a grotesque parody of the people it had killed. It called out to them in Tom's voice, then Mike's, then in voices they didn't recognize but that chilled them to their core.

The mimicry was so perfect, so haunting, that it caused a wave of confusion and terror to wash over Julia and Alex. They didn't know what was real, what was the creature, and what was just their own minds playing tricks on them.

The creature's claws scraped against the door of the storage room, the sound sending shivers down their spines. Julia clutched her weapon tightly, tears streaming down her face as the reality of their situation sank in. They were outmatched, outsmarted, and they were running out of time.

In the lair, Mike, armed with the knowledge of what they were truly facing, made his way back to the school, determined to save his friends. But as he reached the school's entrance, he heard the creature's mimicry—his own voice, calling out to Julia and Alex from inside.

The chapter ended on a cliffhanger, with Mike bursting into the school just as the creature cornered Julia and Alex in the storage room, its blood-soaked claws reaching out for them. The night was filled with their terrified screams, the true horror of the creature now fully revealed.

Chapter 4

The Monster's Game

Mike's heart pounded in his chest as he entered the school. The familiar walls, once a place of safety and learning, now felt like the twisted corridors of a nightmare. The sound of his own voice echoed eerily through the hallways, mimicked perfectly by the creature that stalked them. It was disorienting, hearing himself call out from different directions, the voices overlapping and creating a dissonant chorus.

The creature was playing with them, leading them deeper into the darkness. It used the voices to confuse and terrorize, separating the group and driving them into deadly traps. The school had become a nightmarish labyrinth, each turn leading them further into the creature's grasp.

Mike moved cautiously, his weapon ready, every muscle tensed for an attack. The darkness seemed to close in around him, the flickering lights casting long, distorted shadows. The creature was out there, somewhere, watching, waiting.

"Julia! Alex!" Mike whispered, but his voice was drowned out by the echoes of his own voice, now twisted and malevolent. He knew he had to find them before the creature did, but the school had become a maze, and the creature knew it better than any of them.

Julia and Alex found themselves in a room they had never seen before—a long, narrow space filled with shattered mirrors. The fragments reflected their fear and despair, creating an endless maze of distorted images. The air was thick with tension, each reflection seeming to move independently, adding to their growing sense of dread.

"Stay close," Alex whispered, his voice trembling.

But the creature's presence was palpable. It was in the room with them, using the mirrors to create the illusion of multiple monsters. They saw glimpses of it in the reflections—its grotesque form shifting and twisting, always just out of sight. The fear was overwhelming, the lines between reality and illusion blurring.

The creature struck from the shadows, its claws slicing through the air with a speed and precision that left them no time to react. Julia barely dodged the attack, her heart pounding as she realized how close she had come to death. The mirrors shattered further as the creature moved, each fragment reflecting its twisted form, creating a kaleidoscope of horror.

They fought to keep their wits about them, but the creature was relentless, its attacks swift and brutal. The room became a nightmare of shattered glass and blood, the creature's presence an overwhelming force that threatened to consume them.

Meanwhile, Mike was being led by the creature's mimicry to the gymnasium. The large, open space was eerily silent, the air heavy with the scent of blood. The floor was slick with it, a grotesque reminder of the massacre that had occurred there. The sight sent a wave of nausea through Mike, but he forced himself to stay focused.

The creature was playing a sadistic game, making noises and creating distractions to lure Mike into traps. Every creak of the floor, every rustle of fabric, was a potential death sentence. The gym became a battleground, the creature using the darkness and the blood-soaked floor to its advantage.

Mike narrowly escaped the creature's attacks, each one coming closer than the last. His body was battered and bleeding, his strength waning. The creature was toying with him, wearing him down, enjoying his fear and desperation. The gym was a twisted playground for the monster, and Mike was its prey.

Julia and Alex, after narrowly escaping the mirror room, stumbled upon the creature's feeding ground in the school's basement. The sight that greeted them was worse than any nightmare. The room was filled with half-eaten bodies, the walls covered in fresh blood. The air was thick with the stench of decay, the smell so overpowering that it made Julia gag.

In the center of the room, the creature was feasting. Its grotesque form was fully revealed now, a mass of twisted limbs, scarred flesh, and gaping maws. It was devouring one of the fallen survivors, tearing into the flesh with a sickening hunger. The sound of bones cracking and flesh tearing filled the air, a grotesque symphony of death.

Julia and Alex froze, the horror of the scene paralyzing them. The creature paused, lifting its head as if sensing their presence. Blood dripped from its maw, its eyes glowing with a malevolent intelligence. It had found them.

The creature's sadistic games continued, driving the survivors to the brink of madness. It isolated them, picking them off one by one, each death more brutal and horrifying than the last. The school, once a place of safety, had become a house of horrors, each room a new nightmare.

Julia was separated from Alex and Mike, forced to face the creature alone. The darkness closed in around her, the creature's mimicry filling her ears with the voices of her loved ones. It called to her in her mother's voice, her father's, even her own, each one a twisted mockery of the people she had lost.

The fear was overwhelming, her mind unraveling as the creature tormented her. She could hear its claws scraping against the walls, feel its hot breath on her neck, but every time she turned, there was nothing there. The creature was playing with her, driving her deeper into despair.

The chapter ended on a chilling cliffhanger, with Julia cornered by the creature in the basement. The darkness closed in around her, the creature's blood-soaked claws reaching out. Her screams echoed through the halls, a final, desperate cry for help that would go unanswered.

Chapter 5

The Final Silence

Julia's breath came in ragged gasps as she fought against the creature in the basement. The darkness pressed in around her, the only light coming from the dim, flickering bulbs overhead. She could feel the creature's hot breath on her neck, its claws slicing through the air as it closed in for the kill.

With a desperate scream, she swung her makeshift weapon—a broken pipe—at the creature. The metal connected with a sickening crunch, and the creature reeled back, blood oozing from a deep gash in its side. But the injury only seemed to enrage it further. It let out a guttural roar, the sound echoing through the basement like the howl of a demon.

Julia backed away, her heart pounding in her chest. She was trapped, with no way out. The creature seemed to sense her fear, to savor it. It toyed with her, its claws grazing her skin, drawing blood but not delivering the final blow. It wanted her to suffer.

Just as the creature prepared to strike, the basement door burst open. Mike and Alex charged in, guns blazing. The bullets tore into the creature, driving it back. For a moment, it seemed like they might have won, but the victory was fleeting. The creature recovered quickly, its wounds closing as if by some dark magic.

"We need to get out of here!" Mike shouted, his voice filled with desperation.

The group retreated deeper into the basement, their footsteps echoing in the narrow corridor. They stumbled upon a hidden room, its entrance concealed behind a stack of old crates. The room was filled with strange symbols and old documents, the air thick with the scent of mildew and decay.

"What is this place?" Julia whispered, her eyes scanning the walls covered in cryptic drawings and notes.

"It looks like someone was studying the creature," Alex said, flipping through the dusty pages of an old journal. "Maybe even trying to control it."

The creature, now enraged and wounded, began to tear through the walls and doors, its claws rending wood and stone like paper. The sound was deafening, the walls trembling with each impact. The room shook, dust and debris falling from the ceiling.

"We're running out of time," Mike said, his voice grim. "We need to figure out how to stop this thing, or we're all dead."

As the creature battered down the final door, Julia found a journal that revealed a dark secret. The creature was not just a mindless beast, but a guardian—an ancient, malevolent force tied to the very foundation of Pine Haven. The town's founders had made a pact with this force, sacrificing their own to protect the town's prosperity. The creature was fulfilling its role as enforcer, ensuring that the pact was honored.

"The creature was drawn here because of the pact," Julia said, her voice trembling with realization. "It's not just killing for survival—it's doing what it was created to do."

Mike and Alex exchanged horrified glances as Julia continued. "The journal says the pact was meant to be renewed every generation. But the last sacrifice wasn't made. The creature is trying to fulfill its purpose."

The group faced a harrowing choice. They could fight a hopeless battle against an unstoppable force, or they could submit to the creature's demands and sacrifice one of their own to save the town.

Determined to end the creature's reign of terror, the group chose to fight. They knew it was a suicide mission, but they had to try. The battle was brutal and bloody. The creature, now fully enraged, tore through the survivors with relentless fury. Blood splattered the walls, screams filled the air, and the creature seemed to grow stronger with each kill, feeding off their fear and pain.

One by one, the group members fell, their deaths gruesome and horrifying. Mike was the first to go, his body torn apart by the creature's claws. Alex fought bravely, but he too was no match for the creature's strength and ferocity. His final scream echoed through the basement as the creature ended his life.

Julia was the last one standing, her body battered and bleeding. She backed into a corner, the creature's eyes locked onto hers. It advanced slowly, savoring the moment, knowing that it had won.

As the creature approached, Julia noticed something strange. The creature hesitated, its claws hovering inches from her throat. It was almost as if it recognized her. And then the truth hit her with the force of a sledgehammer.

The twist was revealed: Julia's family had been directly tied to the original pact. Her ancestors had been the ones to make the deal with the malevolent force, and she was the final sacrifice needed to seal the pact and prevent the force from being unleashed upon the world.

Her death was the key. If she died willingly, the creature would be satisfied, and the town—what little was left of it—would be spared. But if she resisted, the creature would keep killing until it had claimed enough blood to renew the pact.

With tears streaming down her face, Julia understood what she had to do. She lowered her weapon and stepped forward, offering herself to the creature. "Take me," she whispered. "End this."

The creature paused, then slowly reached out with its blood-soaked claws. It wrapped them around Julia, pulling her close. She felt the cold, sharp pain of the claws digging into her flesh, but she didn't resist. She closed her eyes, accepting her fate.

The creature killed her swiftly, mercifully. As her life slipped away, she felt a strange sense of peace. The creature's task was complete. It released her body, letting it fall to the ground. Then, as if satisfied, it retreated into the darkness, leaving the town in eerie silence.

The story ended with Pine Haven in ruins, a hollow shell of its former self. The creature was gone, but the sense of dread remained. The final image was of the town, quiet and empty, with the knowledge that the real horror was only just beginning. For the pact had been renewed, and the cycle of terror would continue, hidden in the shadows, waiting for the next generation.

The Depths Below

Chapter 1

The Whispering Well

The town was a quiet, secluded place, nestled deep within the woods. It was a place where time seemed to stand still, where old traditions and superstitions lingered like the morning mist that clung to the trees. At the center of the town stood an ancient well, a relic of the past, its weathered stones covered in moss and creeping ivy. The well had been sealed for as long as anyone could remember, a heavy stone slab covering its mouth, etched with symbols that no one could decipher.

Hannah, the town's historian, had always been fascinated by the well. She spent her days poring over old documents and records, trying to uncover the secrets of the town's past. But the well remained a mystery, its origins shrouded in legend and fear.

Daniel, a construction worker, had little interest in history. His focus was on the present, on the renovation project he had been hired to oversee. The town council had decided to revitalize the square, and part of that involved cleaning up the area around the well. It was just another job to him, another day's work in a quiet place.

Sheriff Cole, the town's lawman, was a practical man. He didn't believe in ghosts or curses, and he certainly didn't believe in the stories that the old-timers told about the well. To him, it was just a hole in the ground, long since abandoned and forgotten. But this town had a way of making even the most skeptical person question what they knew to be true.

It started with a sound. Daniel was working near the well, clearing away the overgrown brush, when he heard it—a faint whisper, almost imperceptible, drifting up from the depths. He paused, listening, but the sound was gone as quickly as it had come. Shaking his head, he dismissed it as his imagination, the result of too many hours spent under the hot sun.

But the sound lingered in his mind, and later that evening, as he was recounting the day's work to Hannah, he mentioned it. "It was weird," he said, his brow furrowed. "It was like… someone was down there, whispering."

Hannah's curiosity was piqued. She had heard stories about the well, about how people claimed to hear voices coming from it late at night. But those were just tales told to scare children, right? Still, she couldn't shake the feeling that there was something more to it.

As she delved into the town's history, she found disturbing accounts of people vanishing near the well, their disappearances never explained. The dates stretched back centuries, each one accompanied by vague references to strange sounds and inexplicable events. The well, it seemed, had always been a source of fear and mystery in the town.

Meanwhile, Sheriff Cole was dealing with a missing person's case. A local teenager had gone out for a walk and never returned. The parents were frantic, and Cole was doing his best to keep the investigation focused. But as more reports of strange noises and missing pets came in, he couldn't help but feel a growing unease. Could the well be connected? He dismissed the thought as superstition, but the nagging doubt remained.

The renovation project progressed smoothly until the day the well was unsealed. It happened by accident—Daniel's crew was removing some debris when one of the workers dislodged the heavy stone slab covering the well. The slab shifted and, with a groan of ancient stone, toppled into the well with a loud crash.

A foul stench wafted up from the depths, a mix of decay and something far worse. The crew exchanged uneasy glances as the air around them seemed to thicken, the atmosphere suddenly oppressive.

"What the hell is that smell?" one of the workers muttered, covering his nose.

Daniel felt a chill run down his spine. The whispering sound returned, louder this time, a low, guttural murmur that seemed to come from the very earth itself. The workers began to complain of feeling watched, of seeing shadows moving out of the corner of their eyes. Tools went missing, only to be found later, bent and broken.

And then, without warning, the creature emerged.

It happened so fast that no one had time to react. One moment, they were standing around the well, trying to figure out what to do next. The next, something long and twisted shot out of the darkness, wrapping around one of the workers' legs. The man screamed as he was yanked off his feet, dragged across the ground toward the well.

The others tried to pull him back, but the creature was too strong. They watched in horror as the man was lifted into the air, his body flailing as he was pulled into the well. The last thing they saw was his bloodied hand clawing at the edge, his screams echoing off the stone walls before he disappeared into the depths below.

The town was thrown into panic. Word of the attack spread quickly, and soon everyone was talking about the creature that had emerged from the well. People barricaded themselves in their homes, too afraid to venture out after dark. The few who did go out were found the next morning, their bodies mutilated beyond recognition.

Hannah, desperate for answers, continued her research, combing through every old document she could find. Finally, she stumbled upon a journal, written by one of the town's founders. The journal detailed how the well had been built not to provide water, but to trap something—something ancient and malevolent that had terrorized the town in its early days.

The creature, the journal explained, was not of this world. It was a being of darkness, a twisted abomination that fed on blood and fear. The founders had sealed it away, but not before it had claimed the lives of many. Now, with the well unsealed, the creature was free once more.

Sheriff Cole, who had been skeptical of the stories, could no longer deny the truth. He joined Hannah and Daniel in a desperate attempt to confront the creature. They armed themselves with whatever weapons they could find and set out to face the monster, hoping to seal the well once again.

But the creature was far more intelligent and deadly than they had anticipated. It moved through the shadows, silent and swift, its grotesque form barely visible in the darkness. It toyed with them, leading them deeper into the night, until they were completely disoriented.

The group decided to set a trap, using themselves as bait to lure the creature back to the well. They hoped to force it back into the depths and reseal the well before it could escape again. But the plan quickly fell apart when the creature attacked.

It struck with terrifying speed, its claws raking across Daniel's chest, sending him crashing to the ground in a spray of blood. Hannah screamed as the creature lunged at her, its maw opening to reveal rows of jagged teeth. She fired her gun, the bullets tearing into its flesh, but it didn't stop. The creature's strength was monstrous, its resilience terrifying.

The creature's long, twisted limbs lashed out, grabbing Sheriff Cole by the leg and dragging him towards the well. He fired his gun wildly, but the creature was relentless, pulling him closer and closer to the gaping maw of the well. With a final, desperate scream, Cole was yanked into the darkness, his voice echoing as he was swallowed by the abyss.

Hannah, bloodied and terrified, watched in horror as the creature slithered back into the well, dragging its prey with it. The well seemed to pulse with a malevolent energy, the ancient symbols on its stones glowing faintly in the dark. The town was silent, the only sound the soft whispering that now filled the air.

The chapter ended with the well sealed once more, but the knowledge that the creature still lurked below, waiting for the next time it would be unleashed. The town's people were left with a lingering dread, knowing that the terror was far from over.

Chapter 2

The Well's Grip Tightens

The town had always been a quiet, sleepy place, but after the creature's attack, a heavy blanket of fear settled over it. People were afraid to leave their homes, and those who did venture out spoke of hearing whispers on the wind and seeing shadows that moved on their own. It was as if the entire town was holding its breath, waiting for something terrible to happen.

Hannah and Daniel, still shaken by the horror they had witnessed, found little comfort in their own homes. Strange things began to happen—unexplained noises in the dead of night, objects moving on their own, and the ever-present feeling of being watched. The air seemed to crackle with a malevolent energy, as though the creature's presence had seeped into the very walls of their homes.

With Sheriff Cole gone, the town was in chaos. There was no one to maintain order, no one to protect them from the growing terror. Paranoia began to take root, spreading like wildfire. The townspeople eyed each other with suspicion, their fear turning to hysteria as they searched for someone, anyone, to blame.

One night, Hannah was jolted awake by a sound that set her heart racing—a faint scratching at her window. She lay still, listening, her breath caught in her throat. The scratching continued, persistent and deliberate, like nails on glass. Summoning all her courage, she slowly rose from her bed and approached the window.

She pulled back the curtain, but there was nothing there. Just the dark, empty night. Yet the feeling of dread only intensified, the air thick with an unseen presence. Hannah knew she was not alone, even if she couldn't see what was out there.

Across town, Daniel was struggling to sleep. The events of the past days weighed heavily on his mind, and every creak of the house made him jump. Suddenly, he heard something moving in his backyard—a low, shuffling sound, like something dragging itself through the dirt.

Grabbing a flashlight, Daniel cautiously stepped outside. The beam of light cut through the darkness, revealing deep claw marks gouged into the earth. Nearby, he found the mutilated remains of a small animal, its body torn apart with a ferocity that made his stomach churn. The creature had returned, and it was getting closer.

As if in response to the mounting fear, the well began to hum—a low, constant vibration that seemed to resonate through the ground, through the very bones of the town. It was like a heartbeat, growing louder and more insistent, as though the well itself was alive and eager to claim more victims.

The fear in the town reached a fever pitch, turning the people against each other. Paranoia took hold, and soon neighbors were accusing neighbors of harboring the creature or being cursed by it. Fights broke out, homes were ransacked, and in the chaos, the line between friend and foe blurred.

Hannah, desperate to understand what was happening, continued her research. She discovered that the well's influence extended far beyond the physical—it was seeping into their minds, warping their thoughts and driving them to madness. The well was no mere hole in the ground; it was a conduit for something far darker.

Daniel, determined to end the nightmare, tried to rally the remaining townspeople to help him seal the well permanently. But the fear and distrust had taken hold, and no one was willing to help. They were too scared, too convinced that the creature was unstoppable, that it was only a matter of time before it claimed them all.

With no other options, Hannah and Daniel made the decision to confront the creature once more. They armed themselves with whatever they could find—guns, knives, even a sledgehammer—and set out for the well in the dead of night.

As they approached, the well seemed to breathe, the hum growing louder and the air thick with a foul, almost tangible presence. It was as if the well itself was alive, pulsing with a dark energy that made their skin crawl.

And then, from the depths of the well, the creature emerged.

Its full form was visible in the moonlight, and it was more horrifying than anything they could have imagined. Long, sinewy limbs stretched out from its twisted body, its skin slick and glistening like the flesh of something that had never seen the light of day. Its face was almost human, but horribly deformed, with hollow eyes that seemed to stare straight into their souls. Its mouth, lined with sharp, bloodstained teeth, opened in a grotesque grin.

The creature let out a low, guttural growl, a sound that reverberated through the night, sending a shiver down their spines. They knew, without a doubt, that they were facing something far beyond their understanding.

The creature attacked with a speed and ferocity that took them by surprise. It moved like a shadow, silent and swift, its claws slashing through the air with deadly precision. The fight was brutal, the air filled with the sounds of growls and screams as Hannah and Daniel struggled to survive.

Desperation fueled their efforts, and they managed to lure the creature back towards the well. But it quickly became clear that the creature was toying with them, enjoying their terror. It would let them think they were gaining the upper hand, only to strike with renewed vigor, leaving them bloodied and battered.

As they neared the well, the creature revealed its true power—a chilling ability to control the minds of those nearby. Hannah suddenly found herself surrounded by figures from her past, long-dead loved ones calling out to her, begging her to join them. Daniel saw his worst fears realized, his mind filled with images of the creature tearing apart everyone he had ever cared about.

The illusions were so vivid, so real, that it was nearly impossible to distinguish them from reality. The creature was inside their heads, twisting their thoughts, turning their own minds against them.

In a final, desperate act, Hannah and Daniel barely managed to escape with their lives, stumbling away from the well and into the darkness. But the creature's final act of vengeance left them shaken, their sanity hanging by a thread. The well remained open, its dark influence spreading further, tightening its grip on the town and everyone in it.

Chapter 3

The Well's Curse

The town was descending into a nightmare. The air was thick with tension, every shadow a potential threat. The well's influence had grown stronger, and it was as if the town itself was under siege by an unseen force. More people were disappearing, their homes left empty and silent. When they were found, their bodies were mutilated beyond recognition, twisted into grotesque shapes that defied explanation.

Hannah and Daniel were no longer safe, even in daylight. The visions that had once plagued their nights now haunted them during the day as well. They saw glimpses of the creature in every reflection, heard its whispers in every gust of wind. Their minds were slowly unraveling, frayed at the edges by the constant terror that had become their reality.

The well, once a silent sentinel at the town's center, now emanated strange sounds at all hours. Low moans echoed from its depths, whispers that seemed to carry on the wind, and the unmistakable sound of something heavy being dragged along the earth. It was as if the well itself had become a living entity, a vessel for the creature's dark power.

In her desperate search for answers, Hannah uncovered something far more terrifying than she had imagined. The creature wasn't just killing the townspeople—it was possessing them, turning them into mindless puppets to do its bidding. These possessed souls wandered the town during the day, their eyes vacant, their movements slow and unnatural. They didn't speak, didn't react to anything around them, as if they were trapped in a waking nightmare.

But at night, the possessed became something else entirely. They turned aggressive, attacking anyone who crossed their path with a ferocity that was horrifying to witness. Their bodies, once human, were now twisted and contorted, their bones cracking as they moved in ways that defied the natural order.

Daniel and Hannah encountered a group of these possessed townsfolk one evening, their vacant stares and jerky movements sending chills down their spines. The confrontation that followed was brutal and bloody. The possessed were terrifyingly strong, their bodies resilient to pain, their attacks relentless. It was as if the creature was channeling its own dark energy through them, using them as extensions of its own twisted will.

The town's descent into madness was swift and terrifying. As the well's curse spread, the remaining townsfolk began to turn on each other. Accusations of possession flew through the air, leading to violent witch hunts. People were dragged from their homes, beaten, and killed by terrified mobs convinced that they were under the creature's control.

Hannah and Daniel were forced to hide, their once-friendly neighbors now seeing them as enemies. The paranoia had made them targets, and they could do nothing but watch as the town tore itself apart, driven by the well's dark power.

They found refuge in an old, abandoned house on the edge of town, but even there, they were not safe. The whispers followed them, growing louder in the silence of the night. Shadows moved of their own accord, taking on shapes that were all too familiar. It was as if the house itself had been claimed by the creature, its influence seeping into every corner.

In a final, desperate attempt to end the nightmare, Hannah and Daniel decided to return to the well. They knew that this was where the creature's power was strongest, where it had emerged from, and where it needed to be confronted.

As they approached, the ground around the well began to crack and shift, as if the earth itself was alive. The once-solid ground now felt unstable, as though something massive and ancient was moving beneath the surface. They realized with growing horror that the well was not just a gateway—it was the creature's lair, a portal to something far more horrific.

The creature emerged from the well, its form larger and more monstrous than ever before. It was no longer just a creature of flesh and bone; it was something far more nightmarish. Its twisted limbs stretched impossibly long, its body shifting and warping as if reality itself was bending around it. The creature's face was almost human, but horribly deformed, with hollow eyes that seemed to see right through them. Its presence warped the world around it, making the nightmarish visions they had been experiencing bleed into the real world.

The creature attacked with overwhelming force, its monstrous form moving with a speed that defied logic. The battle that ensued was like nothing they had faced before. The creature's ability to manipulate reality turned the world around them into a living nightmare. The ground beneath their feet shifted and cracked, walls appeared where there had been none, and the sky itself seemed to darken and twist in response to the creature's will.

In a terrifying twist, they discovered that the creature could use their own fears and memories against them. It reached into their minds, pulling out their deepest fears and manifesting them as physical threats. Hannah saw visions of her loved ones, twisted and deformed, their faces contorted in pain as they begged for her help. Daniel was confronted by nightmarish creatures from his past, memories twisted into horrifying forms that lunged at him with clawed hands and gnashing teeth.

The creature was toying with them, breaking them down piece by piece. They fought with everything they had, but it was clear that they were outmatched. The creature was too powerful, its connection to the well too strong.

As they fought for their lives, the creature revealed its true purpose. It had no intention of being sealed away again. It had been awakened for a reason, and it wouldn't rest until it had claimed every soul in the town. It was here to finish what it had started centuries ago.

In a final, horrifying moment, the creature lunged at Daniel, its claws wrapping around him with a grip of iron. Hannah watched in helpless terror as the creature dragged him towards the well. Daniel's screams echoed through the night as he was pulled into the darkness, his voice growing fainter and fainter until it was swallowed by the depths below.

Hannah was left alone, surrounded by the horrors the creature had unleashed. The well remained open, its dark influence spreading further, tightening its grip on the town and everyone in it. The night was eerily silent, save for the faint, echoing whispers that seemed to come from everywhere and nowhere all at once.

Chapter 4

The Depths of Despair

The town was a shadow of its former self. With Daniel gone, Hannah was left utterly alone, the weight of the nightmare pressing down on her from all sides. The few remaining inhabitants had either fled in terror or succumbed to madness, their minds broken by the horrors that had been unleashed. The streets were eerily silent, save for the occasional distant scream or the sound of something heavy being dragged along the ground.

Hannah's visions became more intense, blurring the line between reality and nightmare. She couldn't tell what was real anymore. Every shadow seemed to move, every whisper carried the sound of Daniel's voice, calling her name, pleading for help. The well's influence had grown stronger, warping the environment around it. The air was thick with the smell of decay, and the ground pulsed as if it were alive, a sick parody of a heartbeat that matched the rhythm of her own fear.

She was being drawn to the well, whether she wanted to go or not. It was as if an invisible force was pulling her closer, urging her to face whatever horrors awaited below. But she wasn't ready—not yet. The terror was too overwhelming, the sense of doom too great.

As night fell, the town transformed into a playground for the creature. The possessed townsfolk, now fully under its control, roamed the streets with a deadly purpose. They were no longer the mindless puppets Hannah had seen before. Their bodies had become grotesque, twisted into forms that suited the creature's will. Limbs elongated, faces distorted, and eyes glowed with a sinister light.

Hannah was forced to navigate this new horror, hiding from the possessed as they searched for her with blank, hungry eyes. They moved with unnatural grace, their heads jerking sharply as if detecting the slightest sound. She could hear them whispering, their voices overlapping in a discordant symphony that set her teeth on edge.

The town itself began to decay. Buildings crumbled, streets cracked, and the air grew thick with a cloying mist that made it hard to breathe. The sky took on a blood-red hue, casting an eerie glow over the carnage. It was as if the town was being consumed from within, its very essence corrupted by the creature's dark power.

Hannah knew she couldn't run forever. If she was going to end this nightmare, she had to face the creature directly. With no other options, she made the decision to descend into the well, knowing full well that it was a one-way trip.

She armed herself with whatever she could find—a knife, a flashlight, a few old relics she hoped might offer some protection—and made her way to the well. The air around it was thick and oppressive, as if the very atmosphere was pushing her away, trying to keep her from entering. But she pressed on, determined to see this through.

The journey down the well was harrowing. The walls were slick with some foul substance, making it difficult to keep her footing. The deeper she went, the stronger the stench of death became, until it was almost unbearable. The darkness was absolute, broken only by the weak beam of her flashlight, which seemed to flicker in and out, as if struggling to stay lit.

Strange, horrific visions plagued her as she descended. She saw images of the town's past, twisted and corrupted by the creature's influence. Faces of the dead appeared in the walls, their eyes accusing, their mouths silently screaming. The further she went, the more the visions intensified, until she could barely keep her sanity intact.

At the bottom of the well, Hannah found herself in a vast, subterranean cavern—a place that seemed far too large to exist beneath the town. The walls pulsed with a sickening rhythm, like the inside of a living organism. Rivers of blood ran through the cavern, their surfaces churning with the faces of the damned, their eyes wide with eternal torment.

The air was filled with the sounds of wailing souls, their voices blending into a horrifying chorus that echoed off the cavern walls. The ground beneath her feet was soft, almost gelatinous, as if it were made of flesh. She had entered the creature's lair, a nightmare realm that defied all logic and reason.

At the center of the cavern, the creature awaited. It had grown even more monstrous since their last encounter, its body a grotesque amalgamation of twisted flesh and bone, pulsing with a dark energy that made the very air vibrate. It towered over her, its hollow eyes fixed on her with an intensity that made her blood run cold.

The creature spoke, its voice a low, rumbling growl that seemed to come from all around her. It revealed its true nature—a malevolent entity that had fed on the fear and suffering of the town for centuries. It was a being of pure darkness, drawn to the town by the sins of its founders. The well had been its prison, but it was also its gateway, a portal to a world of unimaginable horrors.

"You were never meant to survive," the creature hissed, its voice dripping with malice. "Your blood calls to me, just as it called to your ancestors. You are the last of them, the final key to unlocking my full power."

Hannah's heart raced as the creature's words sank in. Her presence in the town was no accident. She was the last descendant of the town's founders, and her blood was the key to fully unleashing the creature's power. The realization hit her like a sledgehammer—she had been brought here, lured to this place, for one purpose: to complete the ritual that would free the creature from its bonds forever.

The final battle was brutal and horrifying. The creature used its full power to manipulate reality around her, warping the cavern into a twisted reflection of her worst nightmares. She was forced to confront her deepest fears and regrets, each one manifesting as a physical threat that clawed and bit at her with terrifying ferocity.

But Hannah was determined. She knew that the only way to stop the creature was to destroy the well itself, to cut off its connection to the town and the world above. With a final, desperate act of sacrifice, she used the last of her strength to bring down the cavern, causing the walls to collapse and the ground to split open.

The creature roared in fury as the cavern began to crumble around it, its body writhing in agony as it was buried beneath the earth. Hannah felt the ground give way beneath her, and for a moment, she was weightless, suspended in the darkness.

And then, everything went black.

Chapter 5

The Blood of the Innocent

Hannah awoke in the suffocating darkness, her body aching and covered in dust and blood. For a moment, she wasn't sure if she was alive or dead, the crushing weight of the rubble pressing down on her chest making it hard to breathe. But as the pain flooded her senses, she realized that she was still alive—trapped beneath the collapsed cavern, buried deep underground.

The air was thick with dust and the stench of decay, every breath a struggle. She could hear the faint, distant groans of the creature, its voice echoing through the debris. It was still alive, somewhere beneath the rubble, struggling to free itself. The sound sent a shiver down her spine, her hope for survival dwindling with each passing second.

As she lay there, trying to free herself from the twisted remains of the cavern, Hannah was confronted by visions—flashes of the creature's past, as if she were seeing through its eyes. She saw the countless lives it had taken over the centuries, felt the fear and pain of its victims as they were dragged into the well, never to be seen again. It was a horrifying glimpse into the mind of a monster, a mind that had known nothing but death and suffering.

The creature's groans grew louder, more determined, and Hannah felt the ground begin to tremble. Panic surged through her as she realized that the creature was not dead. It was digging its way out from beneath the rubble, driven by a rage that seemed almost unstoppable.

The creature's form was even more grotesque than before, its body a mass of broken bones and torn flesh, twisted and deformed by the collapse. It was a nightmare given form, a beast that refused to die. As it pulled itself free from the debris, Hannah could see the madness in its hollow eyes, a hunger that could never be sated.

She knew she had to act quickly. With the last of her strength, she searched through the debris for anything she could use as a weapon. Her fingers closed around a jagged piece of metal, and she gripped it tightly, knowing that this would be her last stand.

The final confrontation was brutal, the cavern around them collapsing as they fought. The walls crumbled, the ground split open to reveal a yawning abyss below. The creature was relentless, its rage driving it to attack with a ferocity that Hannah could barely withstand. She was badly injured, her blood staining the ground as she struggled to keep the creature at bay.

The creature lunged at her, its claws raking across her flesh, and she screamed in pain, the sound echoing off the walls. But even as the pain threatened to overwhelm her, Hannah fought on, knowing that she couldn't let the creature escape. She had to end this, once and for all.

In a moment of clarity, she realized what she had to do. The only way to truly stop the creature was to sacrifice herself, to drag it down into the abyss with her. It was the only way to ensure that it would never harm anyone again.

With a final, desperate effort, she lured the creature to the edge of the abyss, its grotesque form towering over her as it prepared to strike. She could feel the heat of its breath, the weight of its hatred pressing down on her. This was it—the end.

Just as she was about to throw herself and the creature into the abyss, a sudden, horrifying vision struck her. The creature's true purpose was revealed in a flash of sickening clarity.

The creature was not just a mindless killer; it was a guardian—a twisted, malevolent guardian of something far worse. Buried deep beneath the well, imprisoned for millennia, was an ancient evil that had been sealed away long before the town's founders had built the well. The creature's task had been to keep this evil contained, to ensure that it never escaped into the world above.

The well was not meant to be a prison for the creature, but a seal. By destroying the well, Hannah had inadvertently weakened the seal, allowing the true horror to awaken.

The realization hit her like a punch to the gut. Her sacrifice wouldn't stop the creature; it would serve as the final key to fully unleashing the ancient evil beneath the well. The creature had been guiding her all along, manipulating her actions to bring about this moment.

As the ground beneath her collapsed, Hannah's heart sank. She had been a pawn in a game far more twisted and dangerous than she had ever imagined. The creature's grotesque grin widened as it lunged at her, dragging her towards the abyss. Her screams echoed through the cavern, mixing with the creature's triumphant roar as they both plunged into the darkness below.

The final moments were a blur of pain and terror, the world spinning out of control as they fell deeper and deeper into the abyss. The air grew colder, the darkness thicker, until it was all-consuming. And then, with a final, shuddering gasp, Hannah was gone, swallowed by the void.

Above ground, the town was eerily silent. The well remained open, its dark influence spreading like a cancer through the earth. The blood-red sky loomed overhead, casting long shadows over the empty streets. The ancient evil had begun to awaken, its power growing with each passing moment.

The nightmare was far from over. In fact, it had only just begun.

Whispers in the Shadows

Chapter 1

The First Sightings

The town of Black Hollow had always been a place of quiet solitude. Nestled deep in the shadow of old, crumbling mountains and surrounded by dense, foreboding forests, it was a place where time seemed to move more slowly. The townspeople went about their lives with the steady rhythm of the seasons, their days filled with simple routines and the comfort of familiarity.

But recently, something had changed. A dark cloud had settled over Black Hollow, bringing with it a wave of unexplained suicides. They began innocuously enough—a few tragic deaths here and there, each one shocking but ultimately explained away. But as the weeks passed, the suicides became more frequent, more violent, and more disturbing.

The latest was the most horrifying of all. The body of a young man was found hanging in the middle of the town square, his wrists slashed and his body mutilated in ways that defied explanation. His eyes were wide open, staring into the void with a look of sheer terror that seemed to reach beyond the grave. The sight of it sent shivers down the spines of everyone who saw it, the image burned into their minds like a brand.

Sarah, the town's nurse, had been on duty when the body was discovered. She had seen death before—plenty of it—but nothing like this. There was something deeply wrong, something she couldn't put her finger on, but that gnawed at her insides like a festering wound. The town's people were on edge, their fear palpable in the air.

Tom, a retired soldier who had seen more than his fair share of horrors in his time, was struggling with his own demons. The suicides had stirred something within him, a sense of dread that he couldn't shake. He had been having visions—dark, twisted images that flashed before his eyes, leaving him breathless and shaken. He tried to tell himself it was just his PTSD acting up, but deep down, he knew there was more to it than that.

Marcus, the town's new sheriff, was still trying to find his footing in a place where everyone knew everyone else's business. He had dealt with crime before, but nothing like this. The suicides were tearing the town apart, and he was determined to get to the bottom of it, no matter what it took. But as he dug deeper, he began to uncover things that made his blood run cold—things that couldn't be easily explained away.

The rumors started to spread like wildfire. People whispered about a dark figure that appeared just before each suicide, a shadowy presence that lurked in the corners of their vision, always just out of sight. Those who claimed to have seen it described it as a faceless entity, a shifting, amorphous shape that seemed to be made of darkness itself.

Sarah heard the rumors from some of her patients, survivors who had been found before they could take their own lives. They spoke of seeing something in the shadows, something that filled them with a sense of dread so overwhelming that they couldn't bear to go on living. They couldn't describe what they had seen, not fully, but the fear in their eyes was real, and it sent chills down Sarah's spine.

Tom, already haunted by his own memories, began to suspect that the visions he was seeing were more than just figments of his imagination. He started noticing strange things—shadows that moved when they shouldn't, whispers that seemed to come from nowhere. He tried to brush it off, to tell himself it was just the trauma of his past coming back to haunt him, but it was no use. The fear was too real, too visceral.

Marcus, in his search for answers, began to piece together a pattern from witness reports. Almost every victim had mentioned seeing something before they died, a shadowy figure that appeared out of nowhere, watching them with unseen eyes. The reports were all eerily similar, despite coming from people who had never met each other. It was as if the figure was stalking them, driving them to the brink of madness before pushing them over the edge.

The monster made its first full appearance on a cold, moonless night. It was Sarah who saw it first, though she would later wish she hadn't. She had been working late at the clinic, trying to catch up on paperwork, when she noticed a shadow moving outside the window. At first, she thought it was just a trick of the light, but when she looked closer, she saw it—an amorphous, shifting figure standing just outside, its form indistinct but undeniably there.

For a moment, she was frozen with fear, her heart pounding in her chest. The figure seemed to be staring at her, though it had no eyes, no face. It was just a mass of darkness, but its presence was suffocating, filling her with a sense of dread so intense that she could barely breathe. She felt a sudden, overwhelming urge to end it all, to escape the terror that was clawing at her mind.

But then, as quickly as it had appeared, the figure was gone. Sarah collapsed to the floor, gasping for air, her mind reeling from the encounter. She knew then that the rumors were true—the monster was real, and it was coming for them all.

Tom encountered the monster the next day, though he didn't realize it at first. He was out for a walk, trying to clear his head, when he noticed a shadow moving out of the corner of his eye. He turned to look, but there was nothing there. Shaking his head, he continued on, but the feeling of being watched persisted.

As he walked through the woods on the edge of town, the shadows seemed to grow longer, darker, until they surrounded him completely. And then, out of the darkness, the figure emerged. It was just as the others had described—shapeless, faceless, and utterly terrifying. Tom felt a wave of despair wash over him, a crushing sense of hopelessness that made him want to drop to his knees and give up.

But something inside him fought back. With a roar, he turned and ran, his heart pounding in his ears as he fled the scene. He didn't stop running until he was back in town, gasping for breath, his mind racing. He had seen it—he knew it was real. And he knew that no one in Black Hollow was safe.

Marcus saw the monster that night, as he was driving home from the station. He had been thinking about the case, going over the details in his mind, when he caught sight of something in the rearview mirror. At first, he thought it was a trick of the light, but as he stared, the figure became clearer—a dark, shifting shape that seemed to be watching him from the back seat.

Panic surged through him, and he swerved off the road, the car skidding to a halt in a cloud of dust. When he turned around, the figure was gone, but the feeling of dread remained. He sat there for a long time, trying to calm his racing heart, knowing that whatever this thing was, it was far beyond his understanding.

The monster's influence spread rapidly through the town, like a disease with no cure. The suicides became more frequent, more horrific, each death more gruesome than the last. Bodies were found hanging from trees, lying in pools of blood in their homes, or mutilated beyond recognition. And each time, the monster was there, lurking in the shadows, feeding on their despair.

Sarah tried to save those she could, but it was no use. The victims were too far gone, their minds already shattered by the monster's influence. She began to see the figure everywhere—out of the corner of her eye, in the reflections of mirrors, even in the faces of the people she was trying to help. She couldn't tell what was real anymore, couldn't separate the hallucinations from reality. The fear was constant, gnawing at her sanity.

Tom, desperate to protect his family, began to unravel. The monster haunted him day and night, whispering dark thoughts into his mind, pushing him closer and closer to the edge. He started carrying a gun, convinced that it was the only way to protect himself, but deep down, he knew it wouldn't be enough. The monster was inside him now, a part of him, and there was no escaping it.

Marcus, too, was feeling the strain. The weight of the suicides, the fear in the town, and his own encounters with the monster were taking their toll. He could feel the darkness creeping into his mind, a cold, suffocating presence that made it hard to think, hard to breathe. He knew they were running out of time. If they didn't do something soon, the monster would consume them all.

In a last, desperate attempt to stop the monster, Marcus, Sarah, and Tom came together to devise a plan. They knew they couldn't fight the monster directly—it was too powerful, too insidious. But they hoped that by confronting it, by standing together, they could weaken its hold on the town.

They decided to lure the monster to the old church on the outskirts of town, a place they hoped would give them some kind of advantage. The church had been abandoned for years, its windows boarded up, its walls covered in ivy. It was a place where the light barely touched, where shadows reigned.

As they waited in the darkness, the tension was palpable. The air was thick with fear, each of them haunted by their own doubts and fears. They could feel the monster's presence, closing in around them, its whispers filling their minds with dark thoughts.

When the monster finally appeared, it was worse than they had imagined. It was no longer just a shadowy figure—it was a living nightmare, a mass of darkness and despair that seemed to suck the very light from the room. Its form was constantly shifting, a chaotic blend of twisted limbs and featureless voids. But its gaze—its gaze was what broke them.

The moment they locked eyes with the monster, they were lost. The fear, the despair, the overwhelming urge to end it all was too much to bear. The monster used their deepest fears against them, twisting their thoughts, driving them to the brink of suicide. Marcus saw the faces of the people he had failed, their accusing eyes staring back at him. Sarah saw her patients, their bodies twisted and broken, their eyes filled with blame. Tom saw the faces of his comrades, those he had lost, their voices screaming at him to join them.

The monster was winning. They could feel it tightening its grip, pulling them closer and closer to the edge. But just as all hope seemed lost, something inside them sparked. A faint, flickering light, a memory of who they were, of the people they were fighting for.

With a final, desperate surge of strength, they fought back, pushing the monster's influence out of their minds. The effort was excruciating, but slowly, the darkness began to recede. The monster's form wavered, its grip on them loosening.

But as they regained control, the realization hit them like a sledgehammer. The monster wasn't just trying to kill them—it was feeding on them, growing stronger with each second they resisted. And now, it was more powerful than ever.

The chapter ended with the church collapsing around them, the walls crumbling as the monster unleashed its full power. Marcus, Sarah, and Tom were left battered and broken, their victory fleeting as they realized the true horror of their situation: the monster was unstoppable, and it was only a matter of time before it claimed them all.

Chapter 2

The Shadow's Grip Tightens

The night after the confrontation in the church, Black Hollow was a town suffocating under the weight of fear. The survivors of that harrowing encounter were left shattered, their minds reeling from the horror they had faced. The town itself felt different—darker, as though the very air had thickened with dread.

Sarah, Marcus, and Tom each retreated to the supposed safety of their homes, but there was no refuge to be found. The shadows that had haunted them in the church seemed to follow them, lurking in every corner, growing longer and darker with every passing hour. It was as if the monster had left a piece of itself behind, a stain that could never be washed away.

The suicides continued with a terrifying frequency. Each new death was more gruesome than the last, a twisted display of hopelessness that left the entire community shaken. The bodies were found in alleys, in homes, hanging from trees—each face frozen in a rictus of terror that spoke of the horrors they had seen in their final moments. The town was unraveling, and there was nothing anyone could do to stop it.

As the monster's influence grew stronger, it began to manipulate reality itself. Sarah, Marcus, and Tom found themselves trapped in a waking nightmare, unable to trust their own senses. The hallucinations started small—fleeting shadows, whispers just on the edge of hearing—but they quickly escalated into something far more terrifying.

Sarah's encounters with the monster were particularly brutal. She would look into a mirror and see not her own reflection, but a twisted, broken version of herself—her skin pale and bloodied, her eyes sunken and hollow. The reflection would smile at her, a grotesque, mocking grin, and whisper dark thoughts into her mind, thoughts that she couldn't shake no matter how hard she tried.

Marcus wasn't faring much better. He started hearing voices—accusations, taunts, the voices of the dead blaming him for their deaths. They whispered that he had failed, that he was the reason so many had died, that he would never escape the monster's grasp. The guilt weighed heavily on him, and he began to crack under the pressure, his once-steady demeanor giving way to paranoia and fear.

Tom, already fragile from his battles with PTSD, was the first to fall. The monster exploited his memories of war, twisting them into horrific visions that pushed him closer and closer to the edge. He saw the faces of his fallen comrades, their bodies broken and bloodied, accusing him of abandoning them. He heard their screams in the dead of night, felt their hands grabbing at him, pulling him down into the darkness.

One night, Tom finally snapped. The weight of his guilt, combined with the monster's relentless assault on his mind, proved too much to bear. He was found the next morning, his body hanging from a tree in the town square, his wrists slashed, his eyes wide open in terror. His death was a devastating blow to Sarah and Marcus, who were now more isolated and afraid than ever.

The monster fed on Tom's despair, growing even stronger. The shadows in Black Hollow grew thicker, darker, and the sense of doom that pervaded the town became almost unbearable. It was as if the town itself was dying, consumed by the darkness that had taken root in its heart.

With Tom gone, Sarah and Marcus were left to face the monster's growing power on their own. The hallucinations became more frequent, more disturbing, leaving them both on the brink of madness. Every shadow seemed to conceal a lurking threat, every whisper carried the monster's voice, urging them to give in, to end their suffering.

Marcus became paranoid, convinced that the monster was controlling the minds of everyone in town. He started seeing threats where there were none, lashing out at anyone who got too close. His once-rational mind was unraveling, the weight of the monster's influence driving him to the edge.

Sarah, too, was struggling to maintain her sanity. The monster preyed on her deepest fears, her darkest insecurities, showing her visions of her loved ones, their faces twisted and broken, urging her to end her life. The guilt, the despair, the overwhelming sense of hopelessness became too much to bear, and she began to doubt her own sanity, to wonder if there was any point in continuing to fight.

In a last-ditch effort to reclaim their lives, Sarah and Marcus decided to confront the monster one last time. They knew they were running out of time—the monster's influence was too strong, and they were losing their grip on reality. If they didn't act soon, they would end up like Tom, or worse.

They returned to the church, hoping that the sacred ground would give them some protection against the creature. But the church was no longer a sanctuary—it was a graveyard, a place where the dead whispered their despair into the night. The air was thick with the stench of decay, the walls stained with the memories of the night before.

When the monster finally revealed itself, it was more terrifying than anything they could have imagined. It was no longer just a shadowy figure—it was a living embodiment of despair, a mass of writhing shadows and tortured faces, a physical manifestation of the darkness that had consumed the town. The faces of its victims, twisted and broken, stared back at them from the creature's shifting form, their eyes filled with pain and hopelessness.

The monster began to close in, its tendrils of darkness reaching out to ensnare them. Its whispers filled their minds, drowning out all thoughts of hope, leaving them teetering on the edge of madness. The shadows closed in, and they realized that their final stand may be their last.

Chapter 3

Descent into Darkness

The night after the failed confrontation in the church, Black Hollow fell into complete chaos. The monster's influence had spread like a virus, infecting the minds of everyone it touched. Fear and despair took root in the hearts of the town's people, driving them to madness, and those who weren't already lost were soon to follow.

Sarah and Marcus were barely holding onto their sanity. The faces of the dead haunted them relentlessly, their twisted forms appearing in every shadow, their voices carried on the wind like a twisted lullaby. The monster was growing stronger, feeding off the terror and hopelessness that had taken hold of the town.

The suicides became more frequent, more public, more grotesque. Bodies were found hanging from trees in the town square, sprawled across the steps of the courthouse, and lying in pools of blood in the middle of the street. Each death was a message, a testament to the monster's power and the inevitability of their fate.

The town itself seemed to come alive under the monster's influence. The buildings creaked and groaned as if they were in pain, the windows shattered without warning, and the air was thick with a suffocating, oppressive energy that made it hard to breathe. The streets were empty, but the silence was deafening, broken only by the occasional scream or the distant echo of a door slamming shut.

Sarah and Marcus wandered through the streets, searching for some sign of life, some sign that there was still hope. But all they found was death. The townsfolk had turned on each other, driven mad by paranoia and fear. Fights broke out in the middle of the street, and the bodies of those who lost were left where they fell, their blood staining the cobblestones.

They tried to seek help, to find someone who could join them in their fight against the monster, but they were met with hostility and violence. The monster had turned the town into a twisted labyrinth, a living nightmare from which there was no escape.

The monster was toying with them, pushing them closer and closer to the brink of insanity. It created nightmarish illusions, twisting familiar places into horrifying death traps. The town had become a playground for the creature, a place where it could feed on their fear and despair, where it could break them down, piece by piece.

Sarah was lured into an old, abandoned house, a place she had known since childhood. But the house was no longer the safe haven she remembered—it was a place of nightmares. The walls bled, the floors creaked under the weight of something unseen, and the air was filled with the sound of whispers, voices urging her to end her life. She could feel the monster's presence, lurking just out of sight, waiting for her to fall.

Marcus found himself trapped in a hall of mirrors, the reflections warping and twisting into grotesque parodies of himself. Each mirror showed a different version of his own death—hanging from a rope, bleeding out from a self-inflicted wound, lying lifeless in a pool of blood. The monster's voice echoed in his mind, convincing him that there was no escape, that his fate was sealed.

Both Sarah and Marcus were pushed to their breaking points. The monster's influence was so strong that they could no longer distinguish between reality and illusion. Every shadow was a threat, every whisper a promise of death. They saw their own demise in every reflection, heard their last breaths in every gust of wind.

Sarah began to lose hope. The visions of her loved ones, twisted and broken, became more frequent, more vivid. They called out to her, begged her to join them, to end her suffering. The urge to give in, to let go, became almost unbearable.

Marcus, too, was at his limit. The weight of the guilt, the constant accusations of the dead, and the horrific visions of his own death were too much to bear. He started to see the monster's logic—to fight was futile, to resist was pointless. The only way to escape the torment was to give in, to let the darkness take him.

In the final moments of the chapter, the monster revealed its true power. It dragged Sarah and Marcus into a twisted version of Black Hollow—a nightmarish mirror of the town, where the streets were lined with the bodies of the dead, where the living were hunted like animals, where the sun never rose, and the darkness reigned supreme.

The monster's voice was everywhere, whispering in their ears, filling their minds with despair. It showed them the faces of its countless victims, people who had once been like them, people who had tried to fight but had failed. It promised them an end to their suffering, an escape from the pain, if they would just let go, if they would just surrender to the darkness.

They stood on the edge of an abyss, looking down into a void filled with the faces of the dead. The monster's voice called to them from the darkness, urging them to take the final step, to end it all. The shadows closed in around them, and they realized that their fight was hopeless, that the darkness would consume them no matter what they did.

The chapter ended with Sarah and Marcus standing on the brink, their minds shattered, their will to fight almost gone. The monster's whispers grew louder, drowning out all other thoughts, as they faced the ultimate choice: fight a hopeless battle or surrender to the darkness.

Chapter 4

The Monster's Embrace

Black Hollow had become a twisted mockery of the town it once was, a place where reality and nightmare merged into one. The streets that Sarah and Marcus once knew had transformed into a maze of horrors, where the rules of time and space no longer applied. Hours stretched into days, yet the sun never rose. The darkness was eternal, a suffocating presence that pressed down on them from all sides.

The dead lined the streets, their eyes hollow and unseeing, yet somehow still filled with a silent, accusing presence. Their mouths moved in unison, whispering the same chilling refrain over and over: "Join us. Join us." The words crawled under Sarah and Marcus's skin, infecting their minds with a deep, gnawing dread.

As they stumbled through the nightmarish landscape, the dead began to move. At first, it was just the slightest twitch, a hand reaching out, a head turning to follow their movements. But soon, the corpses were rising to their feet, animated by the monster's will, their bodies grotesquely mimicking life. Their flesh hung loosely from their bones, and their eyes were empty sockets, but their intent was clear: they were coming for Sarah and Marcus, and they would not stop until they had dragged them into the same despair that had consumed them.

The streets were a battlefield, and the dead were relentless. Sarah and Marcus fought desperately, using whatever they could find to fend off the advancing hordes. But the more they fought, the more the monster's voice taunted them, a cold, mocking whisper in the back of their minds.

"You can't win," the voice said, its tone dripping with malice. "Every step you take only brings you closer to me. Every life you take strengthens my hold. Why fight when you know you'll lose?"

The dead were everywhere, their lifeless hands reaching out to pull them down, their mouths gaping open in silent screams. The streets were slick with blood, the air thick with the stench of decay. The walls of the buildings seemed to close in, twisting and warping as the monster's influence grew stronger.

Sarah and Marcus were exhausted, their bodies battered and bruised, their minds fraying at the edges. They could feel the monster's presence growing, an oppressive weight that threatened to crush them. The town was a labyrinth of horror, a place where the dead ruled and the living were nothing more than prey.

Eventually, the monster led them to the heart of the town—a place that had once been a park, where children had played and families had gathered. But now, it was a place of despair, a twisted reflection of the monster's power.

The trees were made of bones, their branches stretching out like skeletal hands. The fountain, once a source of joy, now spilled blood into the cracked earth. The ground was littered with the remnants of shattered lives—broken toys, torn clothing, photographs of faces long forgotten.

In the center of this hellish landscape stood a massive, black mirror. Its surface rippled like water, reflecting the twisted world around it. The mirror was a gateway, a portal to the monster's true domain, a place where all hope was lost, and all that remained was despair.

Sarah and Marcus were drawn to the mirror, compelled by a force they could not resist. As they stood before it, they saw their own reflections—but not as they were. The images that stared back at them were lifeless, hollow, and broken. They saw themselves as the monster wanted them to be—soulless, empty shells, consumed by the darkness.

The monster finally revealed its true form as it stepped out of the mirror. It was a grotesque, towering figure made of shadows and the souls of the damned, its body constantly shifting and writhing with the faces of those it had consumed. The faces twisted and contorted in agony, their silent screams echoing in the darkness.

The monster's presence was overwhelming, a physical manifestation of despair so intense that it threatened to crush Sarah and Marcus under its weight. It loomed over them, its shadow stretching out to engulf them, its eyes—if it had eyes—boring into their souls.

"You have no choice," the monster said, its voice a chorus of the damned. "You are mine. There is no escape. But I can offer you peace. Oblivion. An end to your suffering. All you have to do is let go."

The monster's words were like poison, seeping into their minds, filling them with a sense of hopelessness so profound that it felt like drowning. The weight of the darkness was unbearable, pressing down on their chests, making it hard to breathe, hard to think.

The monster was not done with them yet. It used its power to create visions tailored to their deepest fears and desires, offering them a final temptation. It showed Sarah a vision of her family, alive and well, their faces filled with love and warmth. They called out to her from beyond the grave, begging her to join them, to be with them again. The sight of them, so close yet so far away, broke her heart.

Marcus saw himself finally free from the guilt and pain that had plagued him for so long. The monster promised him release, an end to the nightmares, a chance to rest. It showed him a world where the dead were at peace, where the screams and accusations had fallen silent. All he had to do was take the final step, to surrender to the darkness.

The temptation was almost irresistible. The monster's influence was so strong that they could feel themselves slipping, their resolve crumbling as the darkness closed in. The visions were so real, so vivid, that it was hard to remember that they were nothing more than illusions, tricks designed to break them.

As the chapter ended, Sarah and Marcus stood on the brink, their hands reaching out toward the mirror, their minds teetering on the edge of surrender. The monster's laughter echoed in their ears, a sound filled with the promise of oblivion, as the shadows swallowed them whole.

Chapter 5

The Final Descent

Sarah and Marcus stood on the brink of oblivion, their hands outstretched toward the mirror, ready to surrender to the darkness that had consumed their world. The monster's whispers were deafening, a relentless tide of despair that threatened to drown out all thoughts of resistance. As they gazed into the mirror, they saw their future—lifeless, empty shells, trapped in the monster's eternal nightmare, forever lost to the shadows.

The temptation to give in was overwhelming. The promise of peace, of an end to their suffering, was so close, so tantalizing. But somewhere deep inside them, a small flicker of hope still burned, refusing to be extinguished. It was a fragile thing, barely more than a spark, but it was enough to keep them from taking that final step.

Just as their fingers were about to touch the surface of the mirror, the ground beneath them began to shake violently. The monster's voice grew louder, more frantic, as if something was threatening its control. The mirror rippled, and then, with a deafening crash, it shattered into a thousand pieces.

The ground split open, revealing a chasm filled with fire and writhing souls. The air was thick with the stench of sulfur and burning flesh, and the screams of the damned echoed through the darkness. The monster's true domain was revealed—a hellish landscape of torment and despair, where the dead were trapped in endless agony.

Sarah and Marcus realized that they had one final chance to fight back, to escape the monster's clutches. They could feel the monster's grip loosening, its power weakening as the chasm widened. Summoning the last of their strength, they resolved to destroy the monster once and for all, even if it meant sacrificing themselves in the process.

The monster, now fully revealed in its grotesque, towering form, lashed out at them with all its fury. Its body was a mass of shadows and tortured souls, constantly shifting and writhing, as if it could barely contain the darkness within. The air was filled with the screams of the damned as the battle began, the ground beneath them shaking and cracking as the chasm continued to widen.

Sarah and Marcus fought desperately, using everything they had to fend off the monster's attacks. They struck out at it with whatever they could find, but it was like fighting a storm, their efforts barely slowing its advance. The battle was brutal and bloody, with the monster drawing on the power of the souls it had consumed to fuel its rage.

Despite their best efforts, the monster was too powerful. It began to overpower them, driving them closer and closer to the edge of the chasm, where the flames of its domain licked at their heels. The heat was unbearable, the air thick with smoke and ash, and they could feel the ground crumbling beneath their feet.

In a moment of clarity, Sarah realized what she had to do. The only way to defeat the monster was to sever its connection to the physical world, to drag it back into the depths of its own hellish domain. She knew what this meant, knew the cost, but there was no other choice.

With a final, desperate cry, Sarah lunged at the monster, wrapping her arms around its shifting form. The monster roared in anger, but before it could react, she threw herself into the chasm, dragging the monster with her. As they fell, the ground began to tremble, and the monster's hold on reality began to weaken, its power waning as it was pulled back into the depths.

Marcus watched in horror as Sarah disappeared into the flames, her scream echoing through the darkness. He was left alone, standing on the edge of the chasm, the ground crumbling beneath him. The heat was unbearable, the flames reaching up toward him, but he couldn't move, couldn't tear his eyes away from the spot where she had fallen.

For a brief moment, it seemed as though the nightmare was finally over. The chasm began to close, the flames dying down, and the monster's voice faded into nothingness. Marcus turned to leave, his body trembling with exhaustion, his mind reeling from the horrors he had witnessed.

But as he took his first step, he saw something that made his blood run cold—Sarah, standing at the edge of the chasm, but not as she was. Her eyes were hollow, her skin pale, and her face twisted into a grotesque smile. There was something wrong, something deeply, terrifyingly wrong.

The plot twist hit Marcus like a sledgehammer: the monster was not destroyed. It had found a new host in Sarah, using her body as a vessel to continue its reign of terror. She was no longer the woman he had fought beside—she was the monster, and its influence was stronger than ever.

The realization was too much to bear. Marcus stumbled back, his heart pounding in his chest, his mind screaming in denial. But the truth was undeniable. The monster had won. It had claimed Sarah, and now it was free to continue its dark work, to spread its influence far beyond Black Hollow.

As the story ended, Marcus was left alone, surrounded by darkness, knowing that the true horror had only just begun. The monster was still out there, wearing the face of the person he had tried to save. And now, he was the last line of defense against the creature that had already taken so much from him.

The shadows closed in around him, and Marcus knew that he would never escape. The monster's laughter echoed in his ears, a sound filled with the promise of more bloodshed, more despair, as the darkness swallowed him whole.

Share Your Thoughts!

Dear Valued Reader,

Thank you for reading our collection of spooky stories for adults. This book is brought to you by **Skriuwer**, a global group dedicated to crafting content that intrigues and provokes thought. Our aim is to transport you into eerie tales that linger in your mind and evoke the timeless allure of the supernatural.

We hope you enjoyed the chilling narratives and spine-tingling moments that we carefully curated for your reading pleasure. Our goal is to provide you with stories that not only entertain but also evoke the thrill and mystery of the unknown, tapping into the primal fears that lie within us all.

Your journey doesn't have to end now that you've finished the book. We consider you an essential part of our community. If you have any comments, questions, or suggestions on how we can enhance this book or ideas for future tales, please reach out to us at **kontakt@skriuwer.com**. Your feedback is invaluable and helps us create even more engaging and thrilling content for you and others.

Did the stories keep you on the edge of your seat? Please leave a review where you purchased the book. Your insights not only inspire us but also guide other readers in discovering and choosing this collection.

Thank you for choosing **Skriuwer**. Let's continue to explore the unknown together.

With Appreciation,
The Skriuwer Team